T0279977

Wilkie Collins's
The Dead Alive

Wilkie Collins in 1874

Wilkie Collins's
The Dead Alive

The Novel, the Case, and Wrongful Convictions

ROB WARDEN

Foreword by Scott Turow

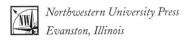

Northwestern University Press
Evanston, Illinois

Northwestern University Press
www.nupress.northwestern.edu

Printed in the United States of America

10 9 8 7 6 5 4 3 2 1

ISBN 0-8101-2294-4

Book design by Marianne Jankowski

Library of Congress Cataloging-in-Publication data are available from
the Library of Congress.

⊗ The paper used in this publication meets the minimum requirements of
the American National Standard for Information Sciences—Permanence
of Paper for Printed Library Materials, ANSI z39.48-1992.

*All proceeds from this book go to the Center on Wrongful Convictions, Bluhm
Legal Clinic, Northwestern University School of Law.*

— CONTENTS —

Wrongful Convictions

— FOREWORD —

Scott Turow

Wilkie Collins—often, and erroneously, credited with inventing the mystery novel—may, on the evidence of *The Dead Alive,* be more appropriately acknowledged as the first author of a legal thriller. *The Dead Alive* has many of the familiar elements of today's subgenre: a lawyer out of sorts with his profession, the legal process gone awry, and a touch of romance to tenderize the rigors of the law. Like many contemporary novels—and those of generations past—*The Dead Alive* probably starts more beguilingly than it ends. But it still displays the stellar craft of a popular novelist with that enigmatic touch of making a story irresistible.

Collins was born in 1824 and was called to the bar in 1851, but like a number of the lawyer-novelists of a century and a half later, he fled the profession in favor of the life of a writer. He became a prolific author of novels, plays, and stories, and his renown sometimes exceeded that of his boon companion—another law office refugee—Charles Dickens. Despite his uncommon success, Collins's life was not especially happy. He never married

<*vii*>

and in his later years became an opium addict. He died in 1879.

Collins's books were referred to as novels of sensation. In the terms of the times, he was the inventor of the "make 'em laugh, make 'em cry, make 'em wait" novel, a literary creation whose qualities of yoking melodrama and keen suspense attracted an enormous following. Collins's most enduring works are *The Woman in White,* whose damsel-in-distress elements are mildly echoed in *The Dead Alive,* and *The Moonstone,* an intricate tale about the search for and recovery of a stolen jewel.

I first read *The Moonstone,* and thus Collins, when I was in my teens, attracted by a paperback cover that called *The Moonstone* the world's first mystery novel. This was apparently based on a remark by T. S. Eliot, who described Collins's work as "the first, the longest and the best of modern English detective novels." Eliot's preeminence cloaked many of his statements about literature with an imposing authority that few questioned. He had once declared, in a review of James Joyce's *Ulysses,* that the book was not a novel since "the novel ended with Flaubert and James," a remark he himself ridiculed nearly forty years later as "absurd." His claim about the provenance of the mystery was equally ill founded, since Edgar Allan Poe's "Murders in the Rue Morgue" had been published more than a quarter of a century before in 1840.

Indeed, for those of us who live in a narrative culture in which the mystery clearly dominates in terms of popularity, it is surprising to think of it as a relatively recent literary development. Theorists have occasionally argued that the Oedipus cycle by Sophocles or Shakespeare's *Macbeth* are mysteries, but surely not in the sense that we now understand the term, as the story of a crime and its investigation. The professional investigation of crime was itself a nineteenth-century development, with the rise of the first urban police departments in Paris and London in 1800 and 1829 respectively. The mystery developed in part to inform those curious about this new profession, although it also reflects a peculiarly modern temperament with its faith in empiricism and technology as the means to divine the enigmas of human intention.

While not the first mystery writer, Collins was one of the true progenitors of the popular novel as we know it today, favoring plots emphasizing sharp emotion and keen suspense over the investigation of character or philosophical rumination. Another popular hallmark of Collins's work, especially in the latter stages of his career, was that it was self-consciously didactic, a trait that led him to be mocked by Swinburne in this doggerel:

What brought good Wilkie's genius nigh perdition?
Some demon whispered—"Wilkie! have a mission."

Unlike high-minded literary types, the reading public did not seem to mind Collins's moralism, nor was its tolerance for learning lessons at the hands of a novelist

<*ix*>

unique to Collins. As the scholar Ian Watt argued long ago in his seminal work *The Rise of the Novel,* the novel has always played an educative role. According to Watt, the initial novel-reading public in the eighteenth century principally comprised middle-class women newly freed from the need to work outside the home and thus looking to the fictional world of *Pamela* and other novels for instruction in how the genteel classes should behave.

Certainly Collins's teaching tendencies are much on display in *The Dead Alive,* clearly meant to lament the quality of what Collins probably regarded as American frontier justice. But like many popular writers before and after him, Collins was still on the nerve in his observations, and his portrayal of how gossip passes itself off as evidence in the eyes of an overwrought community remains an accurate rendition of dozens of wrongful convictions obtained in recent years in this country.

For many reasons, then, *The Dead Alive* deserves our attention today. Gracefully written and artfully suspenseful, it is an early example of the popular novel as we know it now and an eerily prescient forerunner of much of the fiction about the legal process now so widely read in the United States and around the world. More tellingly, its observations remain disturbingly accurate about the factors that can lead the criminal justice system to the wrong conclusions and to the ultimate moral mishap of condemning the innocent to death.

— ACKNOWLEDGMENTS —

The advice and counsel of Gerald W. McFarland, professor of history at the University of Massachusetts in Amherst, was invaluable in the preparation of this book.

Jennifer Linzer, assistant director of the Center on Wrongful Convictions, read and made innumerable and invariably superb suggestions at various stages of the research and writing of the true story behind *The Dead Alive*.

"Other Dead Alive Cases" and "Wrongful Convictions in U.S. Capital Cases" drew heavily on research of wrongful convictions spanning much of the twentieth century by Michael L. Radelet, professor of sociology at the University of Colorado; the late Edwin Borchard, professor of law at Yale University; and the Death Penalty Information Center in Washington, D.C.

Five undergraduate interns at the Center on Wrongful Convictions during the summer of 2004—Kevin Anderson, Kendra Belanger, Michael Feldman, Josh Grossman, and Ryan Wheeler—were immensely helpful in researching and fact-checking details of the cases listed in "Wrongful Convictions in U.S. Capital Cases."

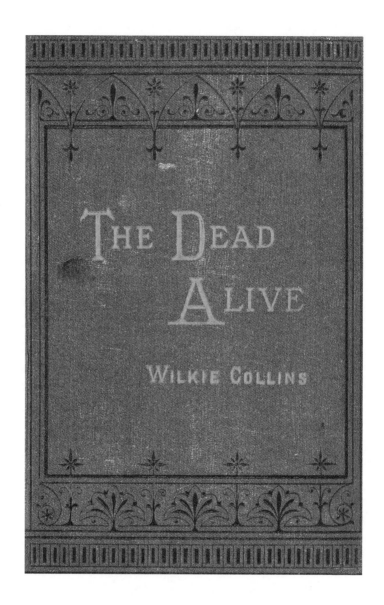

First edition published by Shepard and Gill of Boston in 1874

The Dead Alive

Wilkie Collins

CHAPTER I

The Sick Man

"Heart all right," said the doctor. "Lungs all right. No organic disease that I can discover. Philip Lefrank, don't alarm yourself. You are not going to die yet. The disease you are suffering from is—overwork. The remedy in your case is—rest."

So the doctor spoke, in my chambers in the Temple (London); having been sent for to see me about half an hour after I had alarmed my clerk by fainting at my desk. I have no wish to intrude myself needlessly on the reader's attention; but it may be necessary to add, in the way of explanation, that I am a "junior" barrister in good practice. I come from the Channel Island of Jersey. The French spelling of my name (Lefranc) was Anglicized generations since,—in the days when the letter "k" was still used in England at the end of words which now terminate in "c." We hold our heads high, nevertheless, as a Jersey family. It is to this day a trial to my father to hear his son described as a member of the English bar.

"Rest!" I repeated, when my medical adviser had done. "My good friend, are you aware that it is term-time? The courts are sitting. Look at the briefs waiting for me on that table! Rest means ruin in my case."

"And work," added the doctor quietly, "means death."

I started. He was not trying to frighten me: he was plainly in earnest.

"It is merely a question of time," he went on. "You have a fine constitution; you are a young man: but you cannot deliberately overwork your brain, and derange your nervous system, much longer. Go away at once. If you are a good sailor, take a sea-voyage. The ocean-air is the best of all air to build you up again. No: I don't want to write a prescription. I decline to physic you. I have no more to say."

With these words my medical friend left the room. I was obstinate: I went into court the same day.

The senior counsel in the case on which I was engaged applied to me for some information which it was my duty to give him. To my horror and amazement, I was perfectly unable to collect my ideas: facts and dates all mingled together confusedly in my mind. I was led out of court thoroughly terrified about myself. The next day my briefs went back to the attorneys; and I followed my doctor's advice by taking my passage for America in the first steamer that sailed for New York.

I had chosen the voyage to America in preference to any other trip by sea, with a special object in view. A relative of my mother's had emigrated to the United States many years since, and had thriven there as a farmer. He had given me a general invitation to visit him if I ever crossed the Atlantic. The long period of inaction, under the name of *rest,* to which the doctor's decision had condemned me, could hardly be more pleasantly occupied, as I thought, than by paying a visit to my relation, and seeing what I could of America in that way. After a brief sojourn at New York, I started by railway for the residence of my host,—Mr. Isaac Meadowcroft, of Morwick Farm.

There are some of the grandest natural prospects on the face of creation in America. There is also to be found in certain States of the Union, by way of wholesome contrast, scenery as flat, as monotonous, and as uninteresting to the traveller, as any that the earth can show. The part of the country in which Mr. Meadowcroft's farm was situated fell within this latter category. I looked round me when I stepped out of the railway-carriage on the platform at Morwick Station; and I said to myself, "If to be cured means, in my case, to be dull, I have accurately picked out the very place for the purpose."

I look back at those words by the light of later events; and I pronounce them, as you will soon pronounce them, to be the words of an essentially rash man,

<5>

whose hasty judgment never stopped to consider what surprises time and chance together might have in store for him.

Mr. Meadowcroft's eldest son, Ambrose, was waiting at the station to drive me to the farm.

There was no forewarning, in the appearance of Ambrose Meadowcroft, of the strange and terrible events that were to follow my arrival at Morwick. A healthy, handsome young fellow, one of thousands of other healthy, handsome young fellows, said, "How d'ye do, Mr. Lefrank? Glad to see you, sir. Jump into the buggy: the man will look after your portmanteau." With equally conventional politeness I answered, "Thank you. How are you all at home?" So we started on the way to the farm.

Our conversation on the drive began with the subjects of agriculture and breeding. I displayed my total ignorance of crops and cattle before we had travelled ten yards on our journey. Ambrose Meadowcroft cast about for another topic, and failed to find it. Upon this I cast about on my side, and asked, at a venture, if I had chosen a convenient time for my visit. The young farmer's stolid brown face instantly brightened. I had evidently hit, hap-hazard, on an interesting subject.

"You couldn't have chosen a better time," he said. "Our house has never been so cheerful as it is now."

"Have you any visitors staying with you?"

<6>

"It's not exactly a visitor. It's a new member of the family who has come to live with us."

"A new member of the family! May I ask who it is?"

Ambrose Meadowcroft considered before he replied; touched his horse with the whip; looked at me with a certain sheepish hesitation; and suddenly burst out with the truth, in the plainest possible words:—

"It's just the nicest girl, sir, you ever saw in your life."

"Ay, ay! A friend of your sister's, I suppose?"

"A friend? Bless your heart! it's our little American cousin,—Naomi Colebrook."

I vaguely remembered that a younger sister of Mr. Meadowcroft's had married an American merchant in the remote past, and had died many years since, leaving an only child. I was now further informed that the father also was dead. In his last moments he had committed his helpless daughter to the compassionate care of his wife's relations at Morwick.

"He was always a speculating man," Ambrose went on. "Tried one thing after another, and failed in all. Died, sir, leaving barely enough to bury him. My father was a little doubtful, before she came here, how his American niece would turn out. We are English, you know; and, though we do live in the United States, we stick fast to our English ways and habits. We don't much like American women in general, I can tell you; but, when Naomi made her appearance, she conquered us all.

Such a girl! Took her place as one of the family directly. Learnt to make herself useful in the dairy in a week's time. I tell you this,—she hasn't been with us quite two months yet; and we wonder already how we ever got on without her!"

Once started on the subject of Naomi Colebrook, Ambrose held to that one topic, and talked on it without intermission. It required no great gift of penetration to discover the impression which the American cousin had produced in this case. The young fellow's enthusiasm communicated itself, in a certain tepid degree, to me. I really felt a mild flutter of anticipation at the prospect of seeing Naomi, when we drew up, towards the close of evening, at the gates of Morwick Farm.

< *8* >

CHAPTER II

The New Faces

Immediately on my arrival, I was presented to Mr. Meadowcroft, the father.

The old man had become a confirmed invalid, confined by chronic rheumatism to his chair. He received me kindly, and a little wearily as well. His only unmarried daughter (he had long since been left a widower) was in the room, in attendance on her father. She was a melancholy, middle-aged woman, without visible attractions of any sort,—one of those persons who appear to accept the obligation of living under protest, as a burden which they would never have consented to bear if they had only been consulted first. We three had a dreary little interview in a parlor of bare walls; and then I was permitted to go up stairs, and unpack my portmanteau in my own room.

"Supper will be at nine o'clock, sir," said Miss Meadowcroft.

She pronounced those words as if "supper" was a

<9>

form of domestic offence, habitually committed by the men, and endured by the women. I followed the groom up to my room, not over well pleased with my first experience of the farm.

No Naomi, and no romance, thus far!

My room was clean,—oppressively clean. I quite longed to see a little dust somewhere. My library was limited to the Bible and the Prayer-Book. My view from the window showed me a dead flat in a partial state of cultivation, fading sadly from view in the waning light. Above the head of my spruce white bed hung a scroll, bearing a damnatory quotation from Scripture in emblazoned letters of red and black. The dismal presence of Miss Meadowcroft had passed over my bedroom, and had blighted it. My spirits sank as I looked round me. Supper-time was still an event in the future. I lit the candles, and took from my portmanteau what I firmly believe to have been the first French novel ever produced at Morwick Farm. It was one of the masterly and charming stories of Dumas the elder. In five minutes I was in a new world, and my melancholy room was full of the liveliest French company. The sound of an imperative and uncompromising bell recalled me in due time to the regions of reality. I looked at my watch. Nine o'clock.

Ambrose met me at the bottom of the stairs, and showed me the way to the supper-room.

Mr. Meadowcroft's invalid-chair had been wheeled to the head of the table. On his right-hand side sat his sad and silent daughter. She signed to me, with a ghostly solemnity, to take the vacant place on the left of her father. Silas Meadowcroft came in at the same moment, and was presented to me by his brother. There was a strong family likeness between them, Ambrose being the taller and the handsomer man of the two. But there was no marked character in either face. I set them down as men with undeveloped qualities, waiting (the good and evil qualities alike) for time and circumstances to bring them to their full growth.

The door opened again while I was still studying the two brothers, without, I honestly confess, being very favorably impressed by either of them. A new member of the family-circle, who instantly attracted my attention, entered the room.

He was short, spare, and wiry; singularly pale for a person whose life was passed in the country. The face was in other respects, besides this, a striking face to see. As to the lower part, it was covered with a thick black beard and mustache, at a time when shaving was the rule, and beards the rare exception, in America. As to the upper part of the face, it was irradiated by a pair of wild, glittering brown eyes, the expression of which suggested to me that there was something not quite right with the man's mental balance. A perfectly sane person in all his sayings and doings, so far as I could see, there was still something in those wild brown eyes which suggested to me, that, under exceptionally trying circumstances, he

<11>

might surprise his oldest friends by acting in some exceptionally violent or foolish way. "A little cracked"—that, in the popular phrase, was my impression of the stranger who now made his appearance in the supper-room.

Mr. Meadowcroft the elder, having not spoken one word thus far, himself introduced the new-comer to me, with a side-glance at his sons, which had something like defiance in it,—a glance which, as I was sorry to notice, was returned with the defiance on their side by the two young men.

"Philip Lefrank, this is my overlooker, Mr. Jago," said the old man, formally presenting us. "John Jago, this is my young relative by marriage, Mr. Lefrank. He is not well: he has come over the ocean for rest, and change of scene. Mr. Jago is an American, Philip. I hope you have no prejudice against Americans. Make acquaintance with Mr. Jago. Sit together." He cast another dark look at his sons; and the sons again returned it. They pointedly drew back from John Jago as he approached the empty chair next to me, and moved round to the opposite side of the table. It was plain that the man with the beard stood high in the father's favor, and that he was cordially disliked for that or for some other reason by the sons.

The door opened once more. A young lady quietly joined the party at the supper-table.

Was the young lady Naomi Colebrook? I looked at Ambrose, and saw the answer in his face. Naomi Colebrook at last!

A pretty girl, and, so far as I could judge by appearances, a good girl too. Describing her generally, I may say that she had a small head, well carried, and well set on her shoulders; bright gray eyes, that looked at you honestly, and meant what they looked; a trim, slight little figure,—too slight for our English notions of beauty; a strong American accent; and (a rare thing in America) a pleasantly-toned voice, which made the accent agreeable to English ears. Our first impressions of people are, in nine cases out of ten, the right impressions. I liked Naomi Colebrook at first sight; liked her pleasant smile; liked her hearty shake of the hand when we were presented to each other. "If I get on well with nobody else in this house," I thought to myself, "I shall certainly get on well with *you.*"

For once in a way, I proved a true prophet. In the atmosphere of smouldering enmities at Morwick Farm, the pretty American girl and I remained firm and true friends from first to last.

Ambrose made room for Naomi to sit between his brother and himself. She changed color for a moment, and looked at him, with a pretty, reluctant tenderness, as she took her chair. I strongly suspected the young farmer of squeezing her hand privately, under cover of the tablecloth.

The supper was not a merry one. The only cheerful conversation was the conversation across the table between Naomi and me.

<13>

For some incomprehensible reason, John Jago seemed to be ill at ease in the presence of his young countrywoman. He looked up at Naomi doubtingly from his plate, and looked down again slowly with a frown. When I addressed him, he answered constrainedly. Even when he spoke to Mr. Meadowcroft, he was still on his guard,—on his guard against the two young men, as I fancied by the direction which his eyes took on these occasions. When we began our meal, I had noticed for the first time that Silas Meadowcroft's left hand was strapped up with surgical plaster; and I now further observed that John Jago's wandering brown eyes, furtively looking at everybody round the table in turn, looked with a curious, cynical scrutiny at the young man's injured hand.

By way of making my first evening at the farm all the more embarrassing to me as a stranger, I discovered before long that the father and sons were talking indirectly *at* each other, through Mr. Jago and through me. When old Mr. Meadowcroft spoke disparagingly to his overlooker of some past mistake made in the cultivation of the arable land of the farm, old Mr. Meadowcroft's eyes pointed the application of his hostile criticism straight in the direction of his two sons. When the two sons seized a stray remark of mine about animals in general, and applied it satirically to the mismanagement of sheep and oxen in particular, they looked at John Jago, while they talked to me. On occasions of this sort—and they happened frequently—Naomi struck in resolutely at the right

<14>

moment, and turned the talk to some harmless topic. Every time she took a prominent part in this way in keeping the peace, melancholy Miss Meadowcroft looked slowly round at her in stern and silent disparagement of her interference. A more dreary and more disunited family-party I never sat at the table with. Envy, hatred, malice, and uncharitableness are never so essentially detestable to my mind as when they are animated by a sense of propriety, and work under the surface. But for my interest in Naomi, and my other interest in the little love-looks which I now and then surprised passing between her and Ambrose, I should never have sat through that supper. I should certainly have taken refuge in my French novel and my own room.

At last the unendurably long meal, served with ostentatious profusion, was at an end. Miss Meadowcroft rose with her ghostly solemnity, and granted me my dismissal in these words:—

"We are early people at the farm, Mr. Lefrank. I wish you good-night."

She laid her bony hands on the back of Mr. Meadowcroft's invalid-chair, cut him short in his farewell salutation to me, and wheeled him out to his bed as if she were wheeling him out to his grave.

"Do you go to your room immediately, sir? If not, may I offer you a cigar?—provided the young gentlemen will permit it."

So, picking his words with painful deliberation, and

pointing his reference to "the young gentlemen" with one sardonic side-look at them, Mr. John Jago performed the duties of hospitality on his side. I excused myself from accepting the cigar. With studied politeness, the man of the glittering brown eyes wished me a good night's rest, and left the room.

Ambrose and Silas both approached me hospitably, with their open cigar-cases in their hands.

"You were quite right to say 'No,'" Ambrose began. "Never smoke with John Jago. His cigars will poison you."

"And never believe a word John Jago says to you," added Silas. "He is the greatest liar in America, let the other be whom he may."

Naomi shook her forefinger reproachfully at them, as if the two sturdy young farmers had been two children.

"What will Mr. Lefrank think," she said, "if you talk in that way of a person whom your father respects and trusts? Go and smoke. I am ashamed of both of you."

Silas slunk away without a word of protest. Ambrose stood his ground, evidently bent on making his peace with Naomi before he left her.

Seeing that I was in the way, I walked aside towards a glass door at the lower end of the room. The door opened on the trim little farm-garden, bathed at that moment in lovely moonlight. I stepped out to enjoy the scene, and found my way to a seat under an elm-tree. The grand repose of Nature had never looked so unutterably solemn and beautiful as it now appeared, after what

<16>

I had seen and heard inside the house. I understood, or thought I understood, the sad despair of humanity which led men into monasteries in the old time. The misanthropical side of my nature (where is the sick man who is not conscious of that side of him?) was fast getting the upper hand of me when I felt a light touch laid on my shoulder, and found myself reconciled to my species once more by Naomi Colebrook.

CHAPTER III

The Moonlight-Meeting

"I want to speak to you," Naomi began. "You don't think ill of me for following you out here? We are not accustomed to stand much on ceremony in America."

"You are quite right in America. Pray sit down."

She seated herself by my side, looking at me frankly and fearlessly by the light of the moon.

"You are related to the family here," she resumed, "and I am related too. I guess I may say to *you* what I couldn't say to a stranger. I am right glad you have come here, Mr. Lefrank; and for a reason, sir, which you don't suspect."

"Thank you for the compliment you pay me, Miss Colebrook, whatever the reason may be."

She took no notice of my reply: she steadily pursued her own train of thought.

"I guess you may do some good, sir, in this wretched house," the girl went on, with her eyes still earnestly fixed on my face. "There is no love, no trust, no peace, at Morwick Farm. They want somebody here, except Ambrose. Don't think ill of Ambrose: he is only thoughtless. I say, the rest of them want somebody here to make them ashamed of their hard hearts, and their horrid, false, envious ways. You are a gentleman; you know more than they know: they can't help themselves; they must look up to *you*. Try, Mr. Lefrank, when you have the opportunity,—pray try, sir, to make peace among them. You heard what went on at supper-time; and you were disgusted with it. Oh, yes, you were! I saw you frown to yourself; and I know what *that* means in you Englishmen."

There was no choice but to speak one's mind plainly to Naomi. I acknowledged the impression which had been produced on me at supper-time just as plainly as I have acknowledged it in these pages. Naomi nodded her head in undisguised approval of my candor.

"That will do; that's speaking out," she said. "But— oh, my! you put it a deal too mildly, sir, when you say the men don't seem to be on friendly terms together here. They hate each other. That's the word, Mr. Lefrank,— hate; bitter, bitter, bitter hate!" She clinched her little fists; she shook them vehemently, by way of adding emphasis to her last words; and then she suddenly remembered Ambrose. "Except Ambrose," she added, opening her hand again, and laying it very earnestly on my arm. "Don't go and misjudge Ambrose, sir. There is no harm in poor Ambrose."

The girl's innocent frankness was really irresistible.

"Should I be altogether wrong," I asked, "if I guessed that you were a little partial to Ambrose?"

An Englishwoman would have felt, or would at least have assumed, some little hesitation at replying to my question. Naomi did not hesitate for an instant. "You are quite right, sir," she said with the most perfect composure. "If things go well, I mean to marry Ambrose."

"If things go well," I repeated. "What does that mean? Money?"

She shook her head.

"It means a fear that I have in my own mind," she answered,—"a fear, Mr. Lefrank, of matters taking a bad turn among the men here,—the wicked, hard-hearted, unfeeling men. I don't mean Ambrose, sir: I mean his brother Silas, and John Jago. Did you notice Silas's hand? John Jago did that, sir, with a knife."

"By accident?" I asked.

"On purpose," she answered. "In return for a blow."

This plain revelation of the state of things at Morwick Farm rather staggered me,—blows and knives under the rich and respectable roof-tree of old Mr. Meadowcroft!—blows and knives, not among the laborers, but among the masters! My first impression was like *your* first impression, no doubt. I could hardly believe it.

"Are you sure of what you say?" I inquired.

"I have it from Ambrose. Ambrose would never deceive me. Ambrose knows all about it."

<20>

My curiosity was powerfully excited. To what sort of household had I rashly voyaged across the ocean in search of rest and quiet?

"May I know all about it too?" I said.

"Well, I will try and tell you what Ambrose told me. But you must promise me one thing first, sir. Promise you won't go away and leave us when you know the whole truth. Shake hands on it, Mr. Lefrank; come, shake hands on it."

There was no resisting her fearless frankness. I shook hands on it. Naomi entered on her narrative the moment I had given her my pledge, without wasting a word by way of preface.

"When you are shown over the farm here," she began, "you will see that it is really two farms in one. On this side of it, as we look from under this tree, they raise crops: on the other side—on much the larger half of the land, mind—they raise cattle. When Mr. Meadowcroft got too old and too sick to look after his farm himself, the boys (I mean Ambrose and Silas) divided the work between them. Ambrose looked after the crops, and Silas after the cattle. Things didn't go well, somehow, under their management. I can't tell you why. I am only sure Ambrose was not in fault. The old man got more and more dissatisfied, especially about his beasts. His pride is in his beasts. Without saying a word to the boys, he looked about privately (*I* think he was wrong in that, sir; don't you?)—he looked about privately for help; and, in

<21>

an evil hour, he heard of John Jago. Do you like John Jago, Mr. Lefrank?"

"So far, no. I don't like him."

"Just my sentiments, sir. But I don't know: it's likely we may be wrong. There's nothing against John Jago, except that he is so odd in his ways. They do say he wears all that nasty hair on his face (I hate hair on a man's face) on account of a vow he made when he lost his wife. Don't you think, Mr. Lefrank, a man must be a little mad who shows his grief at losing his wife by vowing that he will never shave himself again? Well, that's what they do say John Jago vowed. Perhaps it's a lie. People are such liars here! Anyway, it's truth (the boys themselves confess *that*), when John came to the farm, he came with a first-rate character. The old father here isn't easy to please; and he pleased the old father. Yes, that's so. Mr. Meadowcroft don't like my countrymen in general. He's like his sons,—English, bitter English, to the marrow of his bones. Somehow, in spite of that, John Jago got round him; maybe because John does certainly know his business. Oh, yes! Cattle and crops, John knows his business. Since he's been overlooker, things have prospered as they didn't prosper in the time of the boys. Ambrose owned as much to me himself. Still, sir, it's hard to be set aside for a stranger; isn't it? John gives the orders now. The boys do their work; but they have no voice in it when John and the old man put their heads together over the business of the farm. I have been long in telling you of it, sir; but now

<22>

you know how the envy and the hatred grew among the men, before my time. Since I have been here, things seem to get worse and worse. There's hardly a day goes by that hard words don't pass between the boys and John, or the boys and their father. The old man has an aggravating way, Mr. Lefrank,—a nasty way, as we do call it,— of taking John Jago's part. Do speak to him about it when you get the chance. The main blame of the quarrel between Silas and John the other day lies at his door, as I think. I don't want to excuse Silas, either. It was brutal of him—though he *is* Ambrose's brother—to strike John, who is the smaller and weaker man of the two. But it was worse than brutal in John, sir, to out with his knife, and try to stab Silas. Oh, he did it! If Silas had not caught the knife in his hand (his hand's awfully cut, I can tell you; I dressed it myself), it might have ended, for any thing I know, in murder"—

She stopped as the word passed her lips, looked back over her shoulder, and started violently.

I looked where my companion was looking. The dark figure of a man was standing, watching us, in the shadow of the elm-tree. I rose directly to approach him. Naomi recovered her self-possession, and checked me before I could interfere.

"Who are you?" she asked, turning sharply towards the stranger. "What do you want there?"

The man stepped out from the shadow into the moonlight, and stood revealed to us as John Jago.

<23>

"I hope I am not intruding?" he said, looking hard at me.

"What do you want?" Naomi repeated.

"I don't wish to disturb you, or to disturb this gentleman," he proceeded. "When you are quite at leisure, Miss Naomi, you would be doing me a favor if you would permit me to say a few words to you in private."

He spoke with the most scrupulous politeness; trying, and trying vainly, to conceal some strong agitation which was in possession of him. His wild brown eyes—wilder than ever in the moonlight—rested entreatingly, with a strange underlying expression of despair, on Naomi's face. His hands, clasped lightly in front of him, trembled incessantly. Little as I liked the man, he did really impress me as a pitiable object at that moment.

"Do you mean that you want to speak to me to-night?" Naomi asked in undisguised surprise.

"Yes, miss, if you please, at your leisure and at Mr. Lefrank's."

Naomi hesitated.

"Won't it keep till to-morrow?" she said.

"I shall be away on farm-business to-morrow, miss, for the whole day. Please to give me a few minutes this evening." He advanced a step towards her: his voice faltered, and dropped timidly to a whisper. "I really have something to say to you, Miss Naomi. It would be a kindness on your part—a very, very great kindness—if you will let me say it before I rest to-night."

<24>

I rose again to resign my place to him. Once more Naomi checked me.

"No," she said. "Don't stir." She addressed John Jago very reluctantly: "If you are so much in earnest about it, Mr. John, I suppose it must be. I can't guess what *you* can possibly have to say to me which cannot be said before a third person. However, it wouldn't be civil, I suppose, to say 'No' in my place. You know it's my business to wind up the hall-clock at ten every night. If you choose to come and help me, the chances are that we shall have the hall to ourselves. Will that do?"

"Not in the hall, miss, if you will excuse me."

"Not in the hall!"

"And not in the house either, if I may make so bold."

"What do you mean?" She turned impatiently, and appealed to me. "Do *you* understand him?"

John Jago sighed to me imploringly to let him answer for himself.

"Bear with me, Miss Naomi," he said. "I think I can make you understand me. There are eyes on the watch, and ears on the watch, in the house; and there are some footsteps—I won't say whose—so soft, that no person can hear them."

The last allusion evidently made itself understood. Naomi stopped him before he could say more.

"Well, where is it to be?" she asked resignedly. "Will the garden do, Mr. John?"

<25>

"Thank you kindly, miss: the garden will do." He pointed to a gravel-walk beyond us, bathed in the full flood of the moonlight. "There," he said, "where we can see all round us, and be sure that nobody is listening. At ten o'clock." He paused, and addressed himself to me. "I beg to apologize, sir, for intruding myself on your conversation. Please to excuse me."

His eyes rested with a last anxious pleading look on Naomi's face. He bowed to us, and melted away into the shadow of the tree. The distant sound of a door closed softly came to us through the stillness of the night. John Jago had re-entered the house.

Now that he was out of hearing, Naomi spoke to me very earnestly:—

"Don't suppose, sir, I have any secrets with *him*," she said. "I know no more than you do what he wants with me. I have half a mind not to keep the appointment when ten o'clock comes. What would you do in my place?"

"Having made the appointment," I answered, "it seems to be due to yourself to keep it. If you feel the slightest alarm, I will wait in another part of the garden, so that I can hear if you call me."

She received my proposal with a saucy toss of the head, and a smile of pity for my ignorance.

"You are a stranger, Mr. Lefrank, or you would never talk to me in that way. In America, we don't do the men the honor of letting them alarm us. In America, the women take care of themselves. He has got my promise

<26>

to meet him, as you say; and I must keep my promise. Only think," she added, speaking more to herself than to me, "of John Jago finding out Miss Meadowcroft's nasty, sly, underhand ways in the house! Most men would never have noticed her."

I was completely taken by surprise. Sad and severe Miss Meadowcroft a listener and a spy! What next at Morwick Farm?

"Was that hint at the watchful eyes and ears, and the soft footsteps, really an allusion to Mr. Meadowcroft's daughter?" I asked.

"Of course it was. Ah! she has imposed on you as she imposes on everybody else. The false wretch! She is secretly at the bottom of half the bad feeling among the men. I am certain of it,—she keeps Mr. Meadowcroft's mind bitter towards the boys. Old as she is, Mr. Lefrank, and ugly as she is, she wouldn't object (if she could only make him ask her) to be John Jago's second wife. No, sir; and she wouldn't break her heart if the boys were not left a stick or a stone on the farm when the father dies. I have watched her, and I know it. Ah! I could tell you such things. But there's no time now,—it's close on ten o'clock: we must say good-night. I am right glad I have spoken to you, sir. I say again, at parting, what I have said already: Use your influence, pray use your influence, to soften them, and to make them ashamed of themselves, in this wicked house. We will have more talk about what you can do, to-morrow, when you are shown over the farm.

I stopped and looked back. They had met.

Say good-by now. Hark! there is ten striking! And look! here is John Jago stealing out again in the shadow of the tree! Good-night, friend Lefrank; and pleasant dreams."

With one hand she took mine, and pressed it cordially: with the other she pushed me away without ceremony in the direction of the house. A charming girl!— an irresistible girl! I was nearly as bad as the boys. I declare, *I* almost hated John Jago, too, as we crossed each other in the shadow of the tree.

Arrived at the glass door, I stopped, and looked back at the gravel-walk.

They had met. I saw the two shadowy figures slowly pacing backwards and forwards in the moonlight, the woman a little in advance of the man. What was he saying to her? Why was he so anxious that not a word of it should be heard? Our presentiments are sometimes, in certain rare cases, the faithful prophecy of the future. A vague distrust of that moonlight-meeting stealthily took a hold on my mind. "Will mischief come of it?" I asked myself as I closed the door and entered the house.

Mischief *did* come of it. You shall hear how.

<29>

CHAPTER IV

The Beechen Stick

Persons of sensitive, nervous temperament, sleeping for the first time in a strange house, and in a bed that is new to them, must make up their minds to pass a wakeful night. My first night at Morwick Farm was no exception to this rule. The little sleep I had was broken and disturbed by dreams. Towards six o'clock in the morning, my bed became unendurable to me. The sun was shining in brightly at the window. I determined to try the reviving influence of a stroll in the fresh morning air.

Just as I got out of bed, I heard footsteps and voices under my window.

The footsteps stopped, and the voices became recognizable. I had passed the night with my window open: I was able, without exciting notice from below, to look out.

The persons beneath me were Silas Meadowcroft, John Jago, and three strangers, whose dress and appearance indicated plainly enough that they were laborers on the farm. Silas was swinging a stout beechen stick in his

<30>

hand, and was speaking to Jago, coarsely and insolently enough, of his moonlight-meeting with Naomi on the previous night.

"Next time you go courting a young lady in secret," said Silas, "make sure that the moon goes down first, or wait for a cloudy sky. You were seen in the garden, Master Jago; and you may as well tell us the truth for once in a way. Did you find her open to persuasion, sir? Did she say 'Yes'?"

John Jago kept his temper.

"If you must have your joke, Mr. Silas," he said quietly and firmly, "be pleased to joke on some other subject. You are quite wrong, sir, in what you suppose to have passed between the young lady and me."

Silas turned about, and addressed himself ironically to the three laborers.

"You hear him, boys? He can't tell the truth, try him as you may. He wasn't making love to Naomi in the garden last night,—oh, dear, no! He has had one wife already; and he knows better than to take the yoke on his shoulders for the second time!"

Greatly to my surprise, John Jago met this clumsy jesting with a formal and serious reply.

"You are quite right, sir," he said. "I have no intention of marrying for the second time. What I was saying to Miss Naomi doesn't matter to you. It was not at all what you choose to suppose: it was something of quite another kind, with which you have no concern. Be pleased to understand once for all, Mr. Silas, that not so much as the thought of making love to the young lady has ever entered my head. I respect her; I admire her good qualities: but if she was the only woman left in the world, and if I was a much younger man than I am, I should never think of asking her to be my wife." He burst out suddenly into a harsh, uneasy laugh. "No, no! not my style, Mr. Silas,—not my style!"

Something in those words, or in his manner of speaking them, appeared to exasperate Silas. He dropped his clumsy irony, and addressed himself directly to John Jago in a tone of savage contempt.

"Not your style?" he repeated. "Upon my soul, that's a cool way of putting it, for a man in your place! What do you mean by calling her 'not your style'? You impudent beggar! Naomi Colebrook is meat for your master!"

John Jago's temper began to give way at last. He approached defiantly a step or two nearer to Silas Meadowcroft.

"Who is my master?" he asked.

"Ambrose will show you, if you go to him," answered the other. "Naomi is *his* sweetheart, not mine. Keep out of his way, if you want to keep a whole skin on your bones."

John Jago cast one of his sardonic side-looks at the farmer's wounded left hand. "Don't forget your own skin, Mr. Silas, when you threaten mine! I have set my mark

on you once, sir. Let me by on my business, or I may
mark you for a second time."

Silas lifted his beechen stick. The laborers, roused
to some rude sense of the serious turn which the quarrel
was taking, got between the two men, and parted them.
I had been hurriedly dressing myself while the altercation
was proceeding; and I now ran down stairs to try what
my influence could do towards keeping the peace at Morwick Farm.

The war of angry words was still going on when I
joined the men outside.

"Be off with you on your business, you cowardly
hound!" I heard Silas say. "Be off with you to the town!
and take care you don't meet Ambrose on the way!"

"Take *you* care you don't feel my knife again before
I go!" cried the other man.

Silas made a desperate effort to break away from the
laborers who were holding him.

"Last time you only felt my fist!" he shouted. "Next
time you shall feel *this*!"

He lifted the stick as he spoke. I stepped up, and
snatched it out of his hand.

"Mr. Silas," I said, "I am an invalid, and I am going
out for a walk. Your stick will be useful to me. I beg leave
to borrow it."

The laborers burst out laughing. Silas fixed his eyes
on me with a stare of angry surprise. John Jago, immedi-

<33>

atcly recovering his self-possession, took off his hat, and made me a deferential bow.

"I had no idea, Mr. Lefrank, that we were disturbing you," he said. "I am very much ashamed of myself, sir. I beg to apologize."

"I accept your apology, Mr. Jago," I answered, "on the understanding that you, as the older man, will set the example of forbearance, if your temper is tried on any future occasion as it has been tried to-day. And I have further to request," I added, addressing myself to Silas, "that you will do me a favor, as your father's guest. The next time your good spirits lead you into making jokes at Mr. Jago's expense, don't carry them quite so far. I am sure you meant no harm, Mr. Silas. Will you gratify me by saying so yourself? I want to see you and Mr. Jago shake hands."

John Jago instantly held out his hand, with an assumption of good feeling which was a little over-acted, to my thinking. Silas Meadowcroft made no advance of the same friendly sort on his side.

"Let him go about his business," said Silas. "I won't waste any more words on him, Mr. Lefrank, to please *you*. But (saving your presence) I'm damned if I take his hand!"

Further persuasion was plainly useless, addressed to such a man as this. Silas gave me no further opportunity of remonstrating with him, even if I had been inclined to do so. He turned about in sulky silence, and, retracing his

<34>

steps along the path, disappeared round the corner of the house. The laborers withdrew next, in different directions, to begin the day's work. John Jago and I were alone.

I left it to the man of the wild brown eyes to speak first.

"In half an hour's time, sir," he said, "I shall be going on business to Narrabee, our market-town here. Can I take any letters to the post for you? or is there any thing else that I can do in the town?"

I thanked him, and declined both proposals. He made me another deferential bow, and withdrew into the house. I mechanically followed the path in the direction which Silas had taken before me.

Turning the corner of the house, and walking on for a little way, I found myself at the entrance to the stables, and face to face with Silas Meadowcroft once more. He had his elbows on the gate of the yard, swinging it slowly backwards and forwards, and turning and twisting a straw between his teeth. When he saw me approaching him, he advanced a step from the gate, and made an effort to excuse himself, with a very ill grace.

"No offence, mister. Ask me what you will besides, and I'll do it for you. But don't ask me to shake hands with John Jago: I hate him too badly for that. If I touched him with one hand, sir, I tell you this, I should throttle him with the other?"

"That's your feeling towards the man, Mr. Silas, is it?"

<35>

"That's my feeling, Mr. Lefrank; and I'm not ashamed of it, either."

"Is there any such place as a church in your neighborhood, Mr. Silas?"

"Of course there is."

"And do you ever go to it?"

"Of course I do."

"At long intervals, Mr. Silas?"

"Every Sunday, sir, without fail."

Some third person behind me burst out laughing; some third person had been listening to our talk. I turned round, and discovered Ambrose Meadowcroft.

"I understand the drift of your catechism, sir, though my brother doesn't," he said. "Don't be hard on Silas, sir. He isn't the only Christian who leaves his Christianity in the pew when he goes out of church. You will never make us friends with John Jago, try as you may. Why, what have you got there, Mr. Lefrank? May I die if it isn't my stick! I have been looking for it everywhere!"

The thick beechen stick had been feeling uncomfortably heavy in my invalid hand for some time past. There was no sort of need for my keeping it any longer. John Jago was going away to Narrabee, and Silas Meadowcroft's savage temper was subdued to a sulky repose. I handed the stick back to Ambrose. He laughed as he took it from me.

"You can't think how strange it feels, Mr. Lefrank, to be out without one's stick," he said. "A man gets used

<36>

to his stick, sir; doesn't he? Are you ready for your breakfast?"

"Not just yet. I thought of taking a little walk first."

"All right, sir. I wish I could go with you; but I have got my work to do this morning, and Silas has his work too. If you go back by the way you came, you will find yourself in the garden. If you want to go farther, the wicket-gate at the end will lead you into the lane."

Through sheer thoughtlessness, I did a very foolish thing. I turned back as I was told, and left the brothers together at the gate of the stable-yard.

<37>

CHAPTER V

The News from Narrabee

Arrived at the garden, a thought struck me. The cheerful speech and easy manner of Ambrose plainly indicated that he was ignorant thus far of the quarrel which had taken place under my window. Silas might confess to having taken his brother's stick, and might mention whose head he had threatened with it. It was not only useless, but undesirable, that Ambrose should know of the quarrel. I retraced my steps to the stable-yard. Nobody was at the gate. I called alternately to Silas and to Ambrose. Nobody answered. The brothers had gone away to their work.

Returning to the garden, I heard a pleasant voice wishing me "Good-morning." I looked round. Naomi Colebrook was standing at one of the lower windows of the farm. She had her working-apron on, and she was industriously brightening the knives for the breakfast-table on an old-fashioned board. A sleek black cat balanced himself on her shoulder, watching the flashing motion of

<38>

A sleek black cat balanced himself on her shoulder.

the knife as she passed it rapidly to and fro on the leather-covered surface of the board.

"Come here," she said: "I want to speak to you."

I noticed, as I approached, that her pretty face was clouded and anxious. She pushed the cat irritably off her shoulder: she welcomed me with only the faint reflection of her bright customary smile.

"I have seen John Jago," she said. "He has been hinting at something which he says happened under your bedroom-window this morning. When I begged him to explain himself, he only answered, 'Ask Mr. Lefrank: I must be off to Narrabee.' What does it mean? Tell me right away, sir! I'm out of temper, and I can't wait!"

Except that I made the best instead of the worst of it, I told her what had happened under my window as plainly as I have told it here. She put down the knife that she was cleaning, and folded her hands before her, thinking.

"I wish I had never given John Jago that meeting," she said. "When a man asks any thing of a woman, the woman, I find, mostly repents it if she says 'Yes.'"

She made that quaint reflection with a very troubled brow. The moonlight-meeting had left some unwelcome remembrances in her mind. I saw that as plainly as I saw Naomi herself.

What had John Jago said to her? I put the question with all needful delicacy, making my apologies beforehand.

"I should like to tell *you*," she began, with a strong emphasis on the last word.

There she stopped. She turned pale; then suddenly flushed again to the deepest red. She took up the knife once more, and went on cleaning it as industriously as ever.

"I mustn't tell you," she resumed, with her head down over the knife. "I have promised not to tell anybody. That's the truth. Forget all about it, sir, as soon as you can. Hush! here's the spy who saw us last night on the walk, and who told Silas!"

Dreary Miss Meadowcroft opened the kitchen-door. She carried an ostentatiously large Prayer-Book; and she looked at Naomi as only a jealous woman of middle age *can* look at a younger and prettier woman than herself.

"Prayers, Miss Colebrook," she said in her sourest manner. She paused, and noticed me standing under the window. "Prayers, Mr. Lefrank," she added, with a look of devout pity, directed exclusively to my address.

"We will follow you directly, Miss Meadowcroft," said Naomi.

"I have no desire to intrude on your secrets, Miss Colebrook."

With that acrid answer, our priestess took herself and her Prayer-Book out of the kitchen. I joined Naomi, entering the room by the garden-door. She met me eagerly.

<41>

"I am not quite easy about something," she said. "Did you tell me that you left Ambrose and Silas together?"

"Yes."

"Suppose Silas tells Ambrose of what happened this morning?"

The same idea, as I have already mentioned, had occurred to my mind. I did my best to re-assure Naomi.

"Mr. Jago is out of the way," I replied. "You and I can easily put things right in his absence."

She took my arm.

"Come in to prayers," she said. "Ambrose will be there, and I shall find an opportunity of speaking to him."

Neither Ambrose nor Silas was in the breakfast-room when we entered it. After waiting vainly for ten minutes, Mr. Meadowcroft told his daughter to read the prayers. Miss Meadowcroft read, thereupon, in the tone of an injured woman taking the throne of mercy by storm, and insisting on her rights. Breakfast followed; and still the brothers were absent. Miss Meadowcroft looked at her father, and said, "From bad to worse, sir. What did I tell you?" Naomi instantly applied the antidote: "The boys are no doubt detained over their work, uncle." She turned to me. "You want to see the farm, Mr. Lefrank. Come and help me to find the boys."

For more than an hour we visited one part of the farm after another, without discovering the missing men.

<42>

We found them at last near the outskirts of a small wood, sitting, talking together, on the trunk of a felled tree.

Silas rose as we approached, and walked away, without a word of greeting or apology, into the wood. As he got on his feet, I noticed that his brother whispered something in his ear; and I heard him answer, "All right."

"Ambrose, does that mean you have something to keep a secret from us?" asked Naomi, approaching her lover with a smile. "Is Silas ordered to hold his tongue?"

Ambrose kicked sulkily at the loose stones lying about him. I noticed, with a certain surprise, that his favorite stick was not in his hand, and was not lying near him.

"Business," he said in answer to Naomi, not very graciously,—"business between Silas and me. That's what it means, if you must know."

Naomi went on, woman-like, with her questions, heedless of the reception which they might meet with from an irritated man.

"Why were you both away at prayers and breakfast-time?" she asked next.

"We had too much to do," Ambrose gruffly replied, "and we were too far from the house."

"Very odd," said Naomi. "This has never happened before since I have been at the farm."

"Well, live and learn. It has happened now."

The tone in which he spoke would have warned any

man to let him alone. But warnings which speak by implication only are thrown away on women. The woman,
having still something in her mind to say, said it.

"Have you seen any thing of John Jago this
morning?"

The smouldering ill temper of Ambrose burst suddenly—why, it was impossible to guess—into a flame.

"How many more questions am I to answer?" he
broke out violently. "Are you the parson, putting me
through my catechism? I have seen nothing of John
Jago, and I have got my work to go on with. Will that do
for you?"

He turned with an oath, and followed his brother
into the wood. Naomi's bright eyes looked up at me, flashing with indignation.

"What does he mean, Mr. Lefrank, by speaking to
me in that way? Rude brute! How dare he do it?" She
paused: her voice, look, and manner suddenly changed.
"This has never happened before, sir. Has any thing gone
wrong? I declare, I shouldn't know Ambrose again, he is
so changed. Say, how does it strike you?"

I still made the best of a bad case.

"Something has upset his temper," I said. "The merest trifle, Miss Colebrook, upsets a man's temper sometimes. I speak as a man, and I know it. Give him time,
and he will make his excuses, and all will be well again."

My presentation of the case entirely failed to re-
assure my pretty companion. We went back to the house.

<44>

Dinner-time came, and the brothers appeared. Their father spoke to them of their absence from morning prayers,—with needless severity, as I thought. They resented the reproof with needless indignation on their side, and left the room. A sour smile of satisfaction showed itself on Miss Meadowcroft's thin lips. She looked at her father; then raised her eyes sadly to the ceiling, and said, "We can only pray for them, sir."

Naomi disappeared after dinner. When I saw her again, she had some news for me.

"I have been with Ambrose," she said, "and he has begged my pardon. We have made it up, Mr. Lefrank. Still—still"—

"Still—*what*, Miss Naomi?"

"He is not like himself, sir. He denies it; but I can't help thinking he is hiding something from me."

The day wore on: the evening came. I returned to my French novel. But not even Dumas himself could keep my attention to the story. What else I was thinking of I cannot say. Why I was out of spirits I am unable to explain. I wished myself back in England: I took a blind unreasoning hatred to Morwick Farm.

Nine o'clock struck; and we all assembled again at supper, with the exception of John Jago. He was expected back to supper; and we waited for him a quarter of an hour, by Mr. Meadowcroft's own directions. John Jago never appeared.

The night wore on, and still the absent man failed

<45>

to return. Miss Meadowcroft volunteered to sit up for him. Naomi eyed her, a little maliciously I must own, as the two women parted for the night. I withdrew to my room; and again I was unable to sleep. When sunrise came, I went out, as before, to breathe the morning air.

On the staircase I met Miss Meadowcroft ascending to her own room. Not a curl of her stiff gray hair was disarranged: nothing about the impenetrable woman betrayed that she had been watching through the night.

"Has Mr. Jago not returned?" I asked.

Miss Meadowcroft slowly shook her head, and frowned at me.

"We are in the hands of Providence, Mr. Lefrank. Mr. Jago must have been detained for the night at Narrabee."

The daily routine of the meals resumed its unalterable course. Breakfast-time came, and dinner-time came, and no John Jago darkened the doors of Morwick Farm. Mr. Meadowcroft and his daughter consulted together, and determined to send in search of the missing man. One of the more intelligent of the laborers was despatched to Narrabee to make inquiries.

The man returned late in the evening, bringing startling news to the farm. He had visited all the inns, and all the places of business resort in Narrabee; he had made endless inquiries in every direction, with this result,—no one had set eyes on John Jago. Everybody declared that John Jago had not entered the town.

We all looked at each other, excepting the two brothers, who were seated together in a dark corner of the room. The conclusion appeared to be inevitable. John Jago was a lost man.

CHAPTER VI

The Lime-Kiln

Mr. Meadowcroft was the first to speak.

"Somebody must find John," he said.

"Without losing a moment," added his daughter.

Ambrose suddenly stepped out of the dark corner of the room.

"*I* will inquire," he said.

Silas followed him.

"I will go with you," he added.

Mr. Meadowcroft interposed his authority.

"One of you will be enough; for the present, at least. Go you, Ambrose. Your brother may be wanted later. If any accident has happened, (which God forbid!) we may have to inquire in more than one direction.—Silas, you will stay at the farm."

The brothers withdrew together; Ambrose to prepare for his journey, Silas to saddle one of the horses for him. Naomi slipped out after them. Left in company

<48>

with Mr. Meadowcroft and his daughter (both devoured by anxiety about the missing man, and both trying to conceal it under an assumption of devout resignation to circumstances), I need hardly add that I, too, retired, as soon as it was politely possible for me to leave the room. Ascending the stairs on my way to my own quarters, I discovered Naomi half hidden by the recess formed by an old-fashioned window-seat on the first landing. My bright little friend was in sore trouble. Her apron was over her face, and she was crying bitterly. Ambrose had not taken his leave as tenderly as usual. She was more firmly persuaded than ever that "Ambrose was hiding something from her." We all waited anxiously for the next day. The next day made the mystery deeper than ever.

The horse which had taken Ambrose to Narrabee was ridden back to the farm by a groom from the hotel. He delivered a written message from Ambrose which startled us. Further inquiries had positively proved that the missing man had never been near Narrabee. The only attainable tidings of his whereabouts were tidings derived from vague report. It was said that a man like John Jago had been seen the previous day in a railway-car, travelling on the line to New York. Acting on this imperfect information, Ambrose had decided on verifying the truth of the report by extending his inquiries to New York.

This extraordinary proceeding forced the suspicion on me that something had really gone wrong. I kept my doubts to myself; but was prepared, from that moment, to see the disappearance of John Jago followed by very grave results.

The same day the results declared themselves.

Time enough had now elapsed for report to spread through the district the news of what had happened at the farm. Already aware of the bad feeling existing between the men, the neighbors had been now informed (no doubt by the laborers present) of the deplorable scene that had taken place under my bedroom-window. Public opinion declares itself in America without the slightest reserve, or the slightest care for consequences. Public opinion declared on this occasion that the lost man was the victim of foul play, and held one or both of the brothers Meadowcroft responsible for his disappearance. Later in the day, the reasonableness of this serious view of the case was confirmed in the popular mind by a startling discovery. It was announced that a Methodist preacher lately settled at Morwick, and greatly respected throughout the district, had dreamed of John Jago in the character of a murdered man, whose bones were hidden at Morwick Farm. Before night the cry was general for a verification of the preacher's dream. Not only in the immediate district, but in the town of Narrabee itself, the public voice insisted on the necessity of a search for the mortal remains of John Jago at Morwick Farm.

In the terrible turn which matters had now taken,

<50>

Mr. Meadowcroft the elder displayed a spirit and an energy for which I was not prepared.

"My sons have their faults," he said, "serious faults; and nobody knows it better than I do. My sons have behaved badly and ungratefully towards John Jago: I don't deny that, either. But Ambrose and Silas are not murderers. Make your search! I ask for it; no, I insist on it, after what has been said, in justice to my family and my name!"

The neighbors took him at his word. The Morwick section of the American nation organized itself on the spot. The sovereign people met in committee, made speeches, elected competent persons to represent the public interests, and began the search the next day. The whole proceeding, ridiculously informal from a legal point of view, was carried on by these extraordinary people with as stern and strict a sense of duty as if it had been sanctioned by the highest tribunal in the land.

Naomi met the calamity that had fallen on the household as resolutely as her uncle himself. The girl's courage rose with the call which was made on it. Her one anxiety was for Ambrose.

"He ought to be here," she said to me. "The wretches in this neighborhood are wicked enough to say that his absence is a confession of his guilt."

She was right. In the present temper of the popular mind, the absence of Ambrose was a suspicious circumstance in itself.

<51>

"We might telegraph to New York," I suggested, "if you only knew where a message would be likely to find him."

"I know the hotel which the Meadowcrofts use at New York," she replied. "I was sent there, after my father's death, to wait till Miss Meadowcroft could take me to Morwick."

We decided on telegraphing to the hotel. I was writing the message, and Naomi was looking over my shoulder, when we were startled by a strange voice speaking close behind us.

"Oh! that's his address, is it?" said the voice. "We wanted his address rather badly."

The speaker was a stranger to me. Naomi recognized him as one of the neighbors.

"What do you want his address for?" she asked sharply.

"I guess we've found the mortal remains of John Jago, miss," the man replied. "We have got Silas already, and we want Ambrose too, on suspicion of murder."

"It's a lie!" cried Naomi furiously,—"a wicked lie!"

The man turned to me.

"Take her into the next room, mister," he said, "and let her see for herself."

We went together into the next room.

In one corner, sitting by her father, and holding his hand, we saw stern and stony Miss Meadowcroft weeping silently. Opposite to them, crouched on the window-

seat,—his eyes wandering, his hands hanging helpless,—we next discovered Silas Meadowcroft, plainly
self-betrayed as a panic-stricken man. A few of the persons who had been engaged in the search were seated
near, watching him. The mass of the strangers present
stood congregated round a table in the middle of the
room. They drew aside as I approached with Naomi, and
allowed us to have a clear view of certain objects placed
on the table.

The centre object of the collection was a little heap
of charred bones. Round this were ranged a knife, two
metal buttons, and a stick partially burnt. The knife was
recognized by the laborers as the weapon John Jago habitually carried about with him,—the weapon with which
he had wounded Silas Meadowcroft's hand. The buttons
Naomi herself declared to have a peculiar pattern on
them, which had formerly attracted her attention to John
Jago's coat. As for the stick, burnt as it was, I had no
difficulty in identifying the quaintly-carved knob at the
top. It was the heavy beechen stick which I had snatched
out of Silas's hand, and which I had restored to Ambrose
on his claiming it as his own. In reply to my inquiries, I
was informed that the bones, the knife, the buttons, and
the stick had all been found together in a lime-kiln then
in use on the farm.

"Is it serious?" Naomi whispered to me as we drew
back from the table.

It would have been sheer cruelty to deceive her now.

"Yes," I whispered back: "it is serious."

The search committee conducted its proceedings with the strictest regularity. The proper applications were made forthwith to a justice of the peace, and the justice issued his warrant. That night Silas was committed to prison; and an officer was despatched to arrest Ambrose in New York.

For my part, I did the little I could to make myself useful. With the silent sanction of Mr. Meadowcroft and his daughter, I went to Narrabee, and secured the best legal assistance for the defence which the town could place at my disposal. This done, there was no choice but to wait for news of Ambrose, and for the examination before the magistrate which was to follow. I shall pass over the misery in the house during the interval of expectation: no useful purpose could be served by describing it now. Let me only say that Naomi's conduct strengthened me in the conviction that she possessed a noble nature. I was unconscious of the state of my own feelings at the time; but I am now disposed to think that this was the epoch at which I began to envy Ambrose the wife whom he had won.

The telegraph brought us our first news of Ambrose. He had been arrested at the hotel, and he was on his way to Morwick. The next day he arrived, and followed his brother to prison. The two were confined in separate cells, and were forbidden all communication with each other.

Two days later, the preliminary examination took place. Ambrose and Silas Meadowcroft were charged before the magistrate with the wilful murder of John Jago. I was cited to appear as one of the witnesses; and, at Naomi's own request, I took the poor girl into court, and sat by her during the proceedings. My host also was present in his invalid-chair, with his daughter by his side.

Such was the result of my voyage across the ocean in search of rest and quiet; and thus did time and chance fulfil my first hasty forebodings of the dull life I was to lead at Morwick Farm!

<55>

CHAPTER VII

The Materials in the Defence

On our way to the chairs allotted to us in the magistrate's court, we passed the platform on which the prisoners were standing together.

Silas took no notice of us. Ambrose made a friendly sign of recognition, and then rested his hand on the "bar" in front of him. As she passed beneath him, Naomi was just tall enough to reach his hand on tiptoe. She took it. "I know you are innocent," she whispered, and gave him one look of loving encouragement as she followed me to her place. Ambrose never lost his self-control. I may have been wrong; but I thought this a bad sign.

The case, as stated for the prosecution, told strongly against the suspected men.

Ambrose and Silas Meadowcroft were charged with the murder of John Jago (by means of the stick or by use of some other weapon), and with the deliberate destruction of the body by throwing it into the quick-lime. In

<56>

proof of this latter assertion, the knife which the deceased habitually carried about him, and the metal buttons which were known to belong to his coat, were produced. It was argued that these indestructible substances, and some fragments of the larger bones, had alone escaped the action of the burning lime. Having produced medical witnesses to support this theory by declaring the bones to be human, and having thus circumstantially asserted the discovery of the remains in the kiln, the prosecution next proceeded to prove that the missing man had been murdered by the two brothers, and had been by them thrown into the quick-lime as a means of concealing their guilt.

Witness after witness deposed to the inveterate enmity against the deceased displayed by Ambrose and Silas. The threatening language they habitually used towards him; their violent quarrels with him, which had become a public scandal throughout the neighborhood, and which had ended (on one occasion at least) in a blow; the disgraceful scene which had taken place under my window; and the restoration to Ambrose, on the morning of the fatal quarrel, of the very stick which had been found among the remains of the dead man,—these facts and events, and a host of minor circumstances besides, sworn to by witnesses whose credit was unimpeachable, pointed with terrible directness to the conclusion at which the prosecution had arrived.

<57>

I looked at the brothers as the weight of the evidence pressed more and more heavily against them. To outward view at least, Ambrose still maintained his self-possession. It was far otherwise with Silas. Abject terror showed itself in his ghastly face; in his great knotty hands, clinging convulsively to the bar at which he stood; in his staring eyes, fixed in vacant horror on each witness who appeared. Public feeling judged him on the spot. There he stood, self-betrayed already, in the popular opinion, as a guilty man!

The one point gained in cross-examination by the defence related to the charred bones.

Pressed on this point, a majority of the medical witnesses admitted that their examination had been a hurried one; and that it was just possible that the bones might yet prove to be the remains of an animal, and not of a man. The presiding magistrate decided upon this that a second examination should be made, and that the number of the medical experts should be increased.

Here the preliminary proceedings ended. The prisoners were remanded for three days.

The prostration of Silas, at the close of the inquiry, was so complete, that it was found necessary to have two men to support him on his leaving the court. Ambrose leaned over the bar to speak to Naomi before he followed the jailer out. "Wait," he whispered confidently, "till they hear what I have to say!" Naomi kissed her hand to him

<58>

affectionately, and turned to me with the bright tears in her eyes.

"Why don't they hear what he has to say at once?" she asked. "Anybody can see that Ambrose is innocent. It's a crying shame, sir, to send him back to prison. Don't you think so yourself?"

If I had confessed what I really thought, I should have said that Ambrose had proved nothing to my mind, except that he possessed rare powers of self-control. It was impossible to acknowledge this to my little friend. I diverted her mind from the question of her lover's innocence by proposing that we should get the necessary order, and visit him in his prison on the next day. Naomi dried her tears, and gave me a little grateful squeeze of the hand.

"Oh, my! what a good fellow you are!" cried the outspoken American girl. "When your time comes to be married, sir, I guess the woman won't repent saying yes to *you!*"

Mr. Meadowcroft preserved unbroken silence as we walked back to the farm on either side of his invalid-chair. His last reserves of resolution seemed to have given way under the overwhelming strain laid on them by the proceedings in court. His daughter, in stern indulgence to Naomi, mercifully permitted her opinion to glimmer on us only through the medium of quotation from Scripture-texts. If the texts meant any thing, they

<59>

meant that she had foreseen all that had happened; and that the one sad aspect of the case, to her mind, was the death of John Jago, unprepared to meet his end.

I obtained the order of admission to the prison the next morning.

We found Ambrose still confident of the favorable result, for his brother and for himself, of the inquiry before the magistrate. He seemed to be almost as eager to tell, as Naomi was to hear, the true story of what had happened at the lime-kiln. The authorities of the prison—present, of course, at the interview—warned him to remember that what he said might be taken down in writing, and produced against him in court.

"Take it down, gentlemen, and welcome," Ambrose replied. "I have nothing to fear: I am only telling the truth."

With that he turned to Naomi, and began his narrative, as nearly as I can remember, in these words:—

"I may as well make a clean breast of it at starting, my girl. After Mr. Lefrank left us that morning, I asked Silas how he came by my stick. In telling me how, Silas also told me of the words that had passed between him and John Jago under Mr. Lefrank's window. I was angry and jealous; and I own it freely, Naomi, I thought the worst that could be thought about you and John."

Here Naomi stopped him without ceremony.

"Was that what made you speak to me as you spoke when we found you at the wood?" she asked.

<60>

"Yes."

"And was that what made you leave me, when you went away to Narrabee, without giving me a kiss at parting?"

"It was."

"Beg my pardon for it before you say a word more."

"I beg your pardon."

"Say you are ashamed of yourself."

"I am ashamed of myself," Ambrose answered penitently.

"Now you may go on," said Naomi. "Now I'm satisfied."

Ambrose went on.

"We were on our way to the clearing at the other side of the wood while Silas was talking to me; and, as ill luck would have it, we took the path that led by the lime-kiln. Turning the corner, we met John Jago on his way to Narrabee. I was too angry, I tell you, to let him pass quietly. I gave him a bit of my mind. His blood was up too, I suppose; and he spoke out, on his side, as freely as I did. I own I threatened him with the stick; but I'll swear to it I meant him no harm. You know—after dressing Silas's hand—that John Jago is ready with his knife. He comes from out West, where they are always ready with one weapon or another handy in their pockets. It's likely enough *he* didn't mean to harm me, either; but how could I be sure of that? When he stepped up to me, and showed his weapon, I dropped the stick, and closed with him.

With one hand I wrenched the knife away from him; and with the other I caught him by the collar of his rotten old coat, and gave him a shaking that made his bones rattle in his skin. A big piece of the cloth came away in my hand. I shied it into the quick-lime close by us, and I pitched the knife after the cloth; and, if Silas hadn't stopped me, I think it's likely I might have shied John Jago himself into the lime next. As it was, Silas kept hold of me. Silas shouted out to him, 'Be off with you! and don't come back again, if you don't want to be burnt in the kiln!' He stood looking at us for a minute, fetching his breath, and holding his torn coat round him. Then he spoke with a deadly-quiet voice and a deadly-quiet look: 'Many a true word, Mr. Silas,' he says, 'is spoken in jest. *I shall not come back again.*' He turned about, and left us. We stood staring at each other like a couple of fools. 'You don't think he means it?' I says. 'Bosh!' says Silas. 'He's too sweet on Naomi not to come back.' What's the matter now, Naomi?"

I had noticed it too. She started and turned pale, when Ambrose repeated to her what Silas had said to him.

"Nothing is the matter," Naomi answered. "Your brother has no right to take liberties with my name. Go on. Did Silas say any more while he was about it?"

"Yes: he looked into the kiln; and he says, 'What made you throw away the knife, Ambrose?' —'How does a man know why he does any thing,' I says, 'when he does it in a passion?'—'It's a ripping-good knife,' says Silas: 'in

<62>

your place, I should have kept it.' I picked up the stick off
the ground. 'Who says I've lost it yet?' I answered him;
and with that I got up on the side of the kiln, and began
sounding for the knife, to bring it, you know, by means
of the stick, within easy reach of a shovel, or some such
thing. 'Give us your hand,' I says to Silas. 'Let me stretch
out a bit, and I'll have it in no time.' Instead of finding
the knife, I came nigh to falling myself into the burning
lime. The vapor overpowered me, I suppose. All I know
is, I turned giddy, and dropped the stick, in the kiln. I
should have followed the stick, to a dead certainty, but
for Silas pulling me back by the hand. 'Let it be,' says
Silas. 'If I hadn't had hold of you, John Jago's knife would
have been the death of you, after all!' He led me away by
the arm, and we went on together on the road to the
wood. We stopped where you found us, and sat down on
the felled tree. We had a little more talk about John Jago.
It ended in our agreeing to wait and see what happened,
and to keep our own counsel in the mean time. You and
Mr. Lefrank came upon us, Naomi, while we were still
talking; and you guessed right when you guessed that we
had a secret from you. You know the secret now."

There he stopped. I put a question to him—the first
that I had asked yet.

"Had you or your brother any fear at the time of the
charge which has since been brought against you?" I said.

"No such thought entered our heads, sir," Ambrose answered. "How could *we* foresee that the neigh-

<63>

bors would search the kiln, and say what they have said of us? All we feared was, that the old man might hear of the quarrel, and be bitterer against us than ever. I was the more anxious of the two to keep things secret, because I had Naomi to consider as well as the old man. Put yourself in my place, and you will own, sir, that the prospect at home was not a pleasant one for *me,* if John Jago really kept away from the farm, and if it came out that it was all my doing."

(This was certainly an explanation of his conduct; but it was not quite satisfactory to my mind.)

"As *you* believe, then," I went on, "John Jago has carried out his threat of not returning to the farm? According to you, he is now alive and in hiding somewhere?"

"Certainly!" said Ambrose.

"Certainly!" repeated Naomi.

"Do you believe the report that he was seen travelling on the railway to New York?"

"I believe it firmly, sir; and, what is more, I believe I was on his track. I was only too anxious to find him; and I say I could have found him, if they would have let me stay in New York."

I looked at Naomi.

"I believe it too," she said. "John Jago is keeping away."

"Do you suppose he is afraid of Ambrose and Silas?"

She hesitated.

"He *may* be afraid of them," she replied, with a strong emphasis on the word "may."

"But you don't think it likely?"

She hesitated again. I pressed her again.

"Do you think there is any other motive for his absence?"

Her eyes dropped to the floor. She answered obstinately, almost doggedly,—

"I can't say."

I addressed myself to Ambrose.

"Have you any thing more to tell us?" I asked.

"No," he said. "I have told you all I know about it."

I rose to speak to the lawyer whose services I had retained. He had helped us to get the order of admission, and he had accompanied us to the prison. Seated apart, he had kept silence throughout, attentively watching the effect of Ambrose Meadowcroft's narrative on the officers of the prison and on me.

"Is this the defence?" I inquired in a whisper.

"This is the defence, Mr. Lefrank. What do you think, between ourselves?"

"Between ourselves, I think the magistrate will commit them for trial."

"On the charge of murder?"

"Yes, on the charge of murder."

CHAPTER VIII

The Confession

My replies to the lawyer accurately expressed the conviction in my mind. The narrative related by Ambrose had all the appearance, in my eyes, of a fabricated story, got up, and clumsily got up, to pervert the plain meaning of the circumstantial evidence produced by the prosecution. I reached this conclusion reluctantly and regretfully, for Naomi's sake. I said all I could say to shake the absolute confidence which she felt in the discharge of the prisoners at the next examination.

The day of the adjourned inquiry arrived.

Naomi and I again attended the court together. Mr. Meadowcroft was unable, on this occasion, to leave the house. His daughter was present, walking to the court by herself, and occupying a seat by herself.

On his second appearance at the "bar," Silas was more composed, and more like his brother. No new witnesses were called by the prosecution. We began the battle over the medical evidence relating to the charred

<66>

bones; and, to some extent, we won the victory. In other words, we forced the doctors to acknowledge that they differed widely in their opinions. Three confessed that they were not certain. Two went still farther, and declared that the bones were the bones of an animal, not of a man. We made the most of this; and then we entered upon the defence, founded on Ambrose Meadowcroft's story.

Necessarily, no witnesses could be called on our side. Whether this circumstance discouraged him, or whether he privately shared my opinion of his client's statement, I cannot say. It is only certain that the lawyer spoke mechanically, doing his best, no doubt, but doing it without genuine conviction or earnestness on his own part. Naomi cast an anxious glance at me as he sat down. The girl's hand, as I took it, turned cold in mine. She saw plain signs of the failure of the defence in the look and manner of the counsel for the prosecution; but she waited resolutely until the presiding magistrate announced his decision. I had only too clearly foreseen what he would feel it to be his duty to do. Naomi's head dropped on my shoulder as he said the terrible words which committed Ambrose and Silas Meadowcroft to take their trial on the charge of murder.

I led her out of the court into the air. As I passed the "bar," I saw Ambrose, deadly pale, looking after us as we left him: the magistrate's decision had evidently daunted him. His brother Silas had dropped in abject terror on the jailer's chair: the miserable wretch shook and shuddered dumbly like a cowed dog.

Miss Meadowcroft returned with us to the farm, preserving unbroken silence on the way back. I could detect nothing in her bearing which suggested any compassionate feeling for the prisoners in her stern and secret nature. On Naomi's withdrawal to her own room, we were left together for a few minutes; and then, to my astonishment, the outwardly merciless woman showed me that she, too, was one of Eve's daughter's, and could feel and suffer, in her own hard way, like the rest of us. She suddenly stepped close up to me, and laid her hand on my arm.

"You are a lawyer, ain't you?" she asked.

"Yes."

"Have you had any experience in your profession?"

"Ten years' experience."

"Do *you* think"—She stopped abruptly; her hard face softened; her eyes dropped to the ground. "Never mind," she said confusedly. "I'm upset by all this misery, though I may not look like it. Don't notice me."

She turned away. I waited, in the firm persuasion that the unspoken question in her mind would sooner or later force its way to utterance by her lips. I was right. She came back to me unwillingly, like a woman acting under some influence which the utmost exertion of her will was powerless to resist.

"Do *you* believe John Jago is still a living man?"

<68>

She put the question vehemently, desperately, as if the words rushed out of her mouth in spite of her.

"I do *not* believe it," I answered.

"Remember what John Jago has suffered at the hands of my brothers," she persisted. "Is it not in your experience that he should take a sudden resolution to leave the farm?"

I replied, as plainly as before,—

"It is *not* in my experience."

She stood looking at me for a moment with a face of blank despair; then bowed her gray head in silence, and left me. As she crossed the room to the door, I saw her look upward; and I heard her say to herself softly, between her teeth, "Vengeance is mine, I will repay, saith the Lord."

It was the requiem of John Jago, pronounced by the woman who loved him.

When I next saw her, her mask was on once more. Miss Meadowcroft was herself again. Miss Meadowcroft could sit by, impenetrably calm, while the lawyers discussed the terrible position of her brothers, with the scaffold in view as one of the possibilities of the "case."

Left by myself, I began to feel uneasy about Naomi. I went up stairs, and, knocking softly at her door, made my inquiries from outside. The clear young voice answered me sadly, "I am trying to bear it: I won't distress you when we meet again." I descended the stairs, feeling my first suspicion of the true nature of my interest in the

<69>

American girl. Why had her answer brought the tears into my eyes? I went out, walking alone, to think undisturbedly. Why did the tones of her voice dwell on my ear all the way? Why did my hand still feel the last cold, faint pressure of her fingers when I led her out of court?

I took a sudden resolution to go back to England.

When I returned to the farm, it was evening. The lamp was not yet lit in the hall. Pausing to accustom my eyes to the obscurity in-doors, I heard the voice of the lawyer whom we had employed for the defence, speaking to some one very earnestly.

"I'm not to blame," said the voice. "She snatched the paper out of my hand before I was aware of her."

"Do you want it back?" asked the voice of Miss Meadowcroft.

"No: it's only a copy. If keeping it will help to quiet her, let her keep it by all means. Good-evening."

Saying these last words, the lawyer approached me on his way out of the house. I stopped him without ceremony: I felt an ungovernable curiosity to know more.

"Who snatched the paper out of your hand?" I asked bluntly.

The lawyer started. I had taken him by surprise. The instinct of professional reticence made him pause before he answered me.

In the brief interval of silence, Miss Meadowcroft replied to my question from the other end of the hall.

<70>

"Naomi Colebrook snatched the paper out of his hand."

"What paper?"

A door opened softly behind me. Naomi herself appeared on the threshold; Naomi herself answered my question.

"I will tell you," she whispered. "Come in here."

One candle only was burning in the room. I looked at her by the dim light. My resolution to return to England instantly became one of the lost ideas of my life.

"Good God!" I exclaimed, "what has happened now?"

She handed me the paper which she had taken from the lawyer's hand.

The "copy" to which he had referred was a copy of the written confession of Silas Meadowcroft on his return to prison. He accused his brother Ambrose of the murder of John Jago. He declared on his oath that he had seen his brother Ambrose commit the crime.

In the popular phrase, I could "hardly believe my own eyes." I read the last sentences of the confession for the second time:—

". . . I heard their voices at the lime-kiln. They were having words about Cousin Naomi. I ran to the place to part them. I was not in time. I saw Ambrose strike the deceased a terrible blow on the head with his (Ambrose's)

<71>

heavy stick. The deceased dropped without a cry. I put my hand on his heart. He was dead. I was horribly frightened. Ambrose threatened to kill *me* next if I said a word to any living soul. He took up the body and cast it into the quick-lime, and threw the stick in after it. We went on together to the wood. We sat down on a felled tree outside the wood. Ambrose made up the story that we were to tell if what he had done was found out. He made me repeat it after him like a lesson. We were still at it when Cousin Naomi and Mr. Lefrank came up to us. They know the rest. This, on my oath, is a true confession. I make it of my own free will, repenting me sincerely that I did not make it before.

(SIGNED) "SILAS MEADOWCROFT."

I laid down the paper, and looked at Naomi once more. She spoke to me with a strange composure. Immovable determination was in her eye; immovable determination was in her voice.

"Silas has lied away his brother's life to save himself," she said. "I see cowardly falsehood and cowardly cruelty in every line on that paper. Ambrose is innocent, and the time has come to prove it."

"You forget," I said, "that we have just failed to prove it."

"John Jago is alive, in hiding from us and from all who know him," she went on. "Help me, friend Lefrank, to advertise for him in the newspapers."

<72>

I saw Ambrose strike the deceased.

I drew back from her in speechless distress. I own I believed that the new misery which had fallen on her had affected her brain.

"You don't believe it," she said. "Shut the door."

I obeyed her. She seated herself, and pointed to a chair near her.

"Sit down," she proceeded. "I am going to do a wrong thing; but there is no help for it. I am going to break a sacred promise. You remember that moonlight-night when I met him on the garden-walk?"

"John Jago?"

"Yes. Now listen. I am going to tell you what passed between John Jago and me."

<74>

— CHAPTER IX —

The Advertisement

I waited in silence for the disclosure that was now to come. Naomi began by asking me a question.

"You remember when we went to see Ambrose in the prison?" she said.

"Perfectly."

"Ambrose told us of something which his villain of a brother said of John Jago and me. Do you remember what it was?"

I remembered perfectly. Silas had said, "John Jago is too sweet on Naomi not to come back."

"That's so," Naomi remarked when I had repeated the words. "I couldn't help starting when I heard what Silas had said; and I thought you noticed me."

"I did notice you."

"Did you wonder what it meant?"

"Yes."

"I'll tell you. It meant this: What Silas Meadow-

<75>

croft said to his brother of John Jago was what I myself was thinking of John Jago at that very moment. It startled me to find my own thought in a man's mind spoken for me by a man. I am the person, sir, who has driven John Jago away from Morwick Farm; and I am the person who can and will bring him back again."

There was something in her manner, more than in her words, which let the light in suddenly on my mind.

"You have told me the secret," I said. "John Jago is in love with you."

"Mad about me!" she rejoined, dropping her voice to a whisper. "Stark, staring mad!—that's the only word for him. After we had taken a few turns on the gravel-walk, he suddenly broke out like a man beside himself. He fell down on his knees; he kissed my gown, he kissed my feet; he sobbed and cried for love of me. I'm not badly off for courage, sir, considering I'm a woman. No man, that I can call to mind, ever really scared me before. But, I own, John Jago frightened me: oh, my! he did frighten me! My heart was in my mouth, and my knees shook under me. I begged and prayed of him to get up and go away. No; there he knelt, and held by the skirt of my gown. The words poured out from him like—well, like nothing I can think of but water from a pump. His happiness and his life, and his hopes in earth and heaven, and Lord only knows what besides, all depended, he

<76>

said, on a word from me. I plucked up spirit enough at that to remind him that I was promised to Ambrose. 'I think you ought to be ashamed of yourself,' I said, 'to own that you're wicked enough to love me when you know I am promised to another man!' When I spoke to him, he took a new turn: he began abusing Ambrose. *That* straightened me up. I snatched my gown out of his hand, and I gave him my whole mind. 'I hate you!' I said. 'Even if I wasn't promised to Ambrose, I wouldn't marry you; no! not if there wasn't another man left in the world to ask me. I hate you, Mr. Jago! I hate you!' He saw I was in earnest at last. He got up from my feet, and he settled down quiet again, all on a sudden. 'You have said enough' (that was how he answered me). 'You have broken my life. I have no hopes and no prospects now. I had a pride in the farm, miss, and a pride in my work; I bore with your brutish cousins' hatred of me; I was faithful to Mr. Meadowcroft's interests; all for your sake, Naomi Colebrook,—all for your sake! I have done with it now; I have done with my life at the farm. You will never be troubled with me again. I am going away, as the dumb creatures go when they are sick, to hide myself in a corner, and die. Do me one last favor. Don't make me the laughing-stock of the whole neighborhood. I can't bear that: it maddens me only to think of it. Give me your promise never to tell any living soul what I have said to you to-night,—your sacred promise

<77>

to the man whose life you have broken!' I did as he bade me: I gave him my sacred promise with the tears in my eyes. Yes, that is so. After telling him I hated him (and I did hate him), I cried over his misery; I did! Mercy, what fools women are! What is the horrid perversity, sir, which makes us always ready to pity the men? He held out his hand to me; and he said, 'Good-by forever!' and I pitied him. I said, 'I'll shake hands with you if you will give me your promise in exchange for mine. I beg of you not to leave the farm. What will my uncle do if you go away? Stay here, and be friends with me, and forget and forgive, Mr. John.' He gave me his promise (he can refuse me nothing); and he gave it again when I saw him again the next morning. Yes, I'll do him justice, though I do hate him! I believe he honestly meant to keep his word as long as my eye was on him. It was only when he was left to himself that the Devil tempted him to break his promise, and leave the farm. I was brought up to believe in the Devil, Mr. Lefrank; and I find it explains many things. It explains John Jago. Only let me find out where he has gone, and I'll engage he shall come back and clear Ambrose of the suspicion which his vile brother has cast on him. Here is the pen all ready for you. Advertise for him, friend Lefrank; and do it right away, for my sake!"

I let her run on, without attempting to dispute her conclusions, until she could say no more. When she put

<78>

the pen into my hand, I began the composition of the advertisement as obediently as if I, too, believed that John Jago was a living man.

In the case of any one else, I should have openly acknowledged that my own convictions remained unshaken. If no quarrel had taken place at the lime-kiln, I should have been quite ready, as I viewed the case, to believe that John Jago's disappearance was referable to the terrible disappointment which Naomi had inflicted on him. The same morbid dread of ridicule which had led him to assert that he cared nothing for Naomi, when he and Silas had quarrelled under my bedroom-window, might also have impelled him to withdraw himself secretly and suddenly from the scene of his discomfiture. But to ask me to believe, after what had happened at the lime-kiln, that he was still living, was to ask me to take Ambrose Meadowcroft's statement for granted as a true statement of facts.

I had refused to do this from the first; and I still persisted in taking that course. If I had been called upon to decide the balance of probability between the narrative related by Ambrose in his defence and the narrative related by Silas in his confession, I must have owned, no matter how unwillingly, that the confession was, to my mind, the least incredible story of the two.

Could I say this to Naomi? I would have written fifty advertisements inquiring for John Jago rather than

<79>

say it; and you would have done the same, if you had been as fond of her as I was.

I drew out the advertisement, for insertion in "The Morwick Mercury," in these terms:—

"MURDER.—Printers of newspapers throughout the United States are desired to publish that Ambrose Meadowcroft and Silas Meadowcroft, of Morwick Farm, Morwick County, are committed for trial on the charge of murdering John Jago, now missing from the farm and from the neighborhood. Any person who can give information of the existence of said Jago may save the lives of two wrongly-accused men by making immediate communication. Jago is about five feet four inches high. He is spare and wiry; his complexion is extremely pale; his eyes are dark, and very bright and restless. The lower part of his face is concealed by a thick, black beard and mustache. The whole appearance of the man is wild and flighty."

I added the date and the address. That evening a servant was sent on horseback to Narrabee to procure the insertion of the advertisement in the next issue of the newspaper.

When we parted that night, Naomi looked almost like her brighter and happier self. Now that the advertisement was on its way to the printing-office, she was more than sanguine: she was certain of the result.

"You don't know how you have comforted me," she said, in her frank, warm-hearted way, when we parted for the night. "All the newspapers will copy it, and we shall hear of John Jago before the week is out." She turned to go, and came back again to me. "I will never forgive Silas for writing that confession!" she whispered in my ear. "If he ever lives under the same roof with Ambrose again, I—well, I believe I wouldn't marry Ambrose if he did! There!"

She left me. Through the wakeful hours of the night my mind dwelt on her last words. That she should contemplate, under any circumstances, even the bare possibility of not marrying Ambrose, was, I am ashamed to say, a direct encouragement to certain hopes which I had already begun to form in secret. The next day's mail brought me a letter on business. My clerk wrote to inquire if there was any chance of my returning to England in time to appear in court at the opening of next law term. I answered, without hesitation, "It is still impossible for me to fix the date of my return." Naomi was in the room while I was writing. How would she have answered, I wonder, if I had told her the truth, and said, "You are responsible for this letter"?

– CHAPTER X –

The Sheriff and the Governor

The question of time was now a serious question at Morwick Farm. In six weeks, the court for the trial of criminal cases was to be opened at Narrabee.

During this interval, no new event of any importance occurred.

Many idle letters reached us relating to the advertisement for John Jago; but no positive information was received. Not the slightest trace of the lost man turned up; not the shadow of a doubt was cast on the assertion of the prosecution, that his body had been destroyed in the kiln. Silas Meadowcroft held firmly to the horrible confession that he had made. His brother Ambrose, with equal resolution, asserted his innocence, and reiterated the statement which he had already advanced. At regular periods I accompanied Naomi to visit him in the prison. As the day appointed for the opening of the court approached, he seemed to falter a little in his resolution; his

<82>

manner became restless; and he grew irritably suspicious about the merest trifles. This change did not necessarily imply the consciousness of guilt: it might merely have indicated natural nervous agitation as the time for the trial drew near. Naomi noticed the alteration in her lover. It greatly increased her anxiety, though it never shook her confidence in Ambrose. Except at meal-times, I was left, during the period of which I am now writing, almost constantly alone with the charming American girl. Miss Meadowcroft searched the newspapers for tidings of the living John Jago in the privacy of her own room. Mr. Meadowcroft would see nobody but his daughter and his doctor, and occasionally one or two old friends. I have since had reason to believe that Naomi, in these days of our intimate association, discovered the true nature of the feeling with which she had inspired me. But she kept her secret. Her manner towards me steadily remained the manner of a sister: she never overstepped by a hair's breadth the safe limits of the character that she had assumed.

The sittings of the court began. After hearing the evidence, and examining the confession of Silas Meadowcroft, the grand jury found a true bill against both the prisoners. The day appointed for their trial was the first day in the new week.

I had carefully prepared Naomi's mind for the decision of the grand jury. She bore the new blow bravely.

<83>

"If you are not tired of it," she said, "come with me to the prison to-morrow. Ambrose will need a little comfort by that time." She paused, and looked at the day's letters lying on the table. "Still not a word about John Jago," she said. "And all the papers have copied the advertisement. I felt so sure we should hear of him long before this!"

"Do you still feel sure that he is living?" I ventured to ask.

"I am as certain of it as ever," she replied firmly. "He is somewhere in hiding: perhaps he is in disguise. Suppose we know no more of him than we know now when the trial begins? Suppose the jury"—She stopped, shuddering. Death—shameful death on the scaffold—might be the terrible result of the consultation of the jury. "We have waited for news to come to us long enough," Naomi resumed. "We must find the tracks of John Jago for ourselves. There is a week yet before the trial begins. Who will help me to make inquiries? Will you be the man, friend Lefrank?"

It is needless to add (though I knew nothing would come of it) that I consented to be the man.

We arranged to apply that day for the order of admission to the prison, and, having seen Ambrose, to devote ourselves immediately to the contemplated search. How that search was to be conducted was more than I could tell, and more than Naomi could tell. We were to begin by applying to the police to help us to find John

<84>

Jago, and we were then to be guided by circumstances. Was there ever a more hopeless programme than this?

"Circumstances" declared themselves against us at starting. I applied, as usual, for the order of admission to the prison, and the order was for the first time refused; no reason being assigned by the persons in authority for taking this course. Inquire as I might, the only answer given was, "Not to-day."

At Naomi's suggestion, we went to the prison to seek the explanation which was refused to us at the office. The jailer on duty at the outer gate was one of Naomi's many admirers. He solved the mystery cautiously in a whisper. The sheriff and the governor of the prison were then speaking privately with Ambrose Meadowcroft in his cell: they had expressly directed that no persons should be admitted to see the prisoner that day but themselves.

What did it mean? We returned, wondering, to the farm. There Naomi, speaking by chance to one of the female servants, made certain discoveries.

Early that morning the sheriff had been brought to Morwick by an old friend of the Meadowcrofts. A long interview had been held between Mr. Meadowcroft and his daughter and the official personage introduced by the friend. Leaving the farm, the sheriff had gone straight to the prison, and had proceeded with the governor to visit Ambrose in his cell. Was some potent influence being brought privately to bear on Ambrose? Appear-

<85>

ances certainly suggested that inquiry. Supposing the influence to have been really exerted, the next question followed, What was the object in view? We could only wait and see.

Our patience was not severely tried. The event of the next day enlightened us in a very unexpected manner. Before noon, the neighbors brought startling news from the prison to the farm.

Ambrose Meadowcroft had confessed himself to be the murderer of John Jago! He had signed the confession in the presence of the sheriff and the governor on that very day!

I saw the document. It is needless to reproduce it here. In substance, Ambrose confessed what Silas had confessed; claiming, however, to have only struck Jago under intolerable provocation, so as to reduce the nature of his offence against the law from murder to manslaughter. Was the confession really the true statement of what had taken place? or had the sheriff and the governor, acting in the interests of the family name, persuaded Ambrose to try this desperate means of escaping the ignominy of death on the scaffold? The sheriff and the governor preserved impenetrable silence until the pressure put on them judicially at the trial obliged them to speak.

Who was to tell Naomi of this last and saddest of all the calamities which had fallen on her? Knowing how I loved her in secret, I felt an invincible reluctance to be the

person who revealed Ambrose Meadowcroft's degrada-
tion to his betrothed wife. Had any other member of the
family told her what had happened? The lawyer was able
to answer me: Miss Meadowcroft had told her.

I was shocked when I heard it. Miss Meadowcroft
was the last person in the house to spare the poor girl:
Miss Meadowcroft would make the hard tidings doubly
terrible to bear in the telling. I tried to find Naomi, without success. She had been always accessible at other times.
Was she hiding herself from me now? The idea occurred
to me as I was descending the stairs after vainly knocking at the door of her room. I was determined to see her.
I waited a few minutes, and then ascended the stairs
again suddenly. On the landing I met her, just leaving
her room.

She tried to run back. I caught her by the arm, and
detained her. With her free hand she held her handkerchief over her face so as to hide it from me.

"You once told me I had comforted you," I said to
her gently. "Won't you let me comfort you now?"

She still struggled to get away, and still kept her
head turned from me.

"Don't you see that I am ashamed to look you in the
face?" she said in low, broken tones. "Let me go."

I still persisted in trying to soothe her. I drew her to
the window-seat. I said I would wait until she was able to
speak to me.

She dropped on the seat, and wrung her hands on her lap. Her downcast eyes still obstinately avoided meeting mine.

"Oh!" she said to herself, "what madness possessed me? Is it possible that I ever disgraced myself by loving Ambrose Meadowcroft?" She shuddered as the idea found its way to expression on her lips. The tears rolled slowly over her cheeks. "Don't despise me, Mr. Lefrank!" she said faintly.

I tried, honestly tried, to put the confession before her in its least unfavorable light.

"His resolution has given way," I said. "He has done this, despairing of proving his innocence, in terror of the scaffold."

She rose, with an angry stamp of her foot. She turned her face on me with the deep-red flush of shame in it, and the big tears glistening in her eyes.

"No more of him!" she said sternly. "If he is not a murderer, what else is he? A liar and a coward! In which of his characters does he disgrace me most? I have done with him forever! I will never speak to him again!" She pushed me furiously away from her; advanced a few steps towards her own door; stopped, and came back to me. The generous nature of the girl spoke in her next words. "I am not ungrateful to *you*, friend Lefrank. A woman in my place is only a woman; and, when she is shamed as I am, she feels it very bitterly. Give me your hand! God bless you!"

She put my hand to her lips before I was aware of her, and kissed it, and ran back into her room.

I sat down on the place which she had occupied. She had looked at me for one moment when she kissed my hand. I forgot Ambrose and his confession; I forgot the coming trial; I forgot my professional duties and my English friends. There I sat, in a fool's elysium of my own making, with absolutely nothing in my mind but the picture of Naomi's face at the moment when she had last looked at me!

I have already mentioned that I was in love with her. I merely add this to satisfy you that I tell the truth.

CHAPTER XI

The Pebble and the Window

Miss Meadowcroft and I were the only representatives of the family at the farm who attended the trial. We went separately to Narrabee. Excepting the ordinary greetings at morning and night, Miss Meadowcroft had not said one word to me since the time when I had told her that I did *not* believe John Jago to be a living man.

I have purposely abstained from encumbering my narrative with legal details. I now propose to state the nature of the defence in the briefest outline only.

We insisted on making both the prisoners plead not guilty. This done, we took an objection to the legality of the proceedings at starting. We appealed to the old English law, that there should be no conviction for murder until the body of the murdered person was found, or proof of its destruction obtained beyond a doubt. We denied that sufficient proof had been obtained in the case now before the court.

<90>

The judges consulted, and decided that the trial should go on.

We took our next objection when the confessions were produced in evidence. We declared that they had been extorted by terror, or by undue influence; and we pointed out certain minor particulars in which the two confessions failed to corroborate each other. For the rest, our defence on this occasion was, as to essentials, what our defence had been at the inquiry before the magistrate. Once more the judges consulted, and once more they overruled our objection. The confessions were admitted in evidence.

On their side, the prosecution produced one new witness in support of their case. It is needless to waste time in recapitulating his evidence. He contradicted himself gravely on cross-examination. We showed plainly, and after investigation proved, that he was not to be believed on his oath.

The chief justice summed up.

He charged, in relation to the confessions, that no weight should be attached to a confession incited by hope or fear; and he left it to the jury to determine whether the confessions in this case had been so influenced. In the course of the trial, it had been shown for the defence that the sheriff and the governor of the prison had told Ambrose, with his father's knowledge and sanction, that the case was clearly against him; that the only chance of spar-

<91>

ing his family the disgrace of his death by public execution lay in making a confession; and that they would do their best, if he did confess, to have his sentence commuted to transportation for life. As for Silas, he was proved to have been beside himself with terror when he made his abominable charge against his brother. We had vainly trusted to the evidence on these two points to induce the court to reject the confessions; and we were destined to be once more disappointed in anticipating that the same evidence would influence the verdict of the jury on the side of mercy. After an absence of an hour, they returned into court with a verdict of "Guilty" against both the prisoners.

Being asked in due form if they had any thing to say in mitigation of their sentence, Ambrose and Silas solemnly declared their innocence, and publicly acknowledged that their respective confessions had been wrung from them by the hope of escaping the hangman's hands. This statement was not noticed by the bench. The prisoners were both sentenced to death.

On my return to the farm, I did not see Naomi. Miss Meadowcroft informed her of the result of the trial. Half an hour later, one of the women-servants handed to me an envelope bearing my name on it in Naomi's handwriting.

The envelope enclosed a letter, and with it a slip of paper on which Naomi had hurriedly written these

<92>

words: "For God's sake, read the letter I send to you, and do something about it immediately!"

I looked at the letter. It assumed to be written by a gentleman in New York. Only the day before, he had, by the merest accident, seen the advertisement for John Jago, cut out of a newspaper and pasted into a book of "curiosities" kept by a friend. Upon this he wrote to Morwick Farm to say that he had seen a man exactly answering to the description of John Jago, but bearing another name, working as a clerk in a merchant's office in Jersey City. Having time to spare before the mail went out, he had returned to the office to take another look at the man before he posted his letter. To his surprise, he was informed that the clerk had not appeared at his desk that day. His employer had sent to his lodgings, and had been informed that he had suddenly packed up his hand-bag after reading the newspaper at breakfast; had paid his rent honestly, and had gone away, nobody knew where!

It was late in the evening when I read these lines. I had time for reflection before it would be necessary for me to act.

Assuming the letter to be genuine, and adopting Naomi's explanation of the motive which had led John Jago to absent himself secretly from the farm, I reached the conclusion that the search for him might be usefully limited to Narrabee and to the surrounding neighborhood.

The newspaper at his breakfast had no doubt given

<93>

him his first information of the "finding" of the grand
jury, and of the trial to follow. It was in my experience of
human nature that he should venture back to Narrabee
under these circumstances, and under the influence of his
infatuation for Naomi. More than this, it was again in
my experience, I am sorry to say, that he should attempt
to make the critical position of Ambrose a means of ex-
torting Naomi's consent to listen favorably to his suit.
Cruel indifference to the injury and the suffering which
his sudden absence might inflict on others was plainly
implied in his secret withdrawal from the farm. The
same cruel indifference, pushed to a farther extreme,
might well lead him to press his proposals privately on
Naomi, and to fix her acceptance of them as the price to
be paid for saving her cousin's life.

To these conclusions I arrived after much thinking.
I had determined, on Naomi's account, to clear the matter up; but it is only candid to add, that my doubts of
John Jago's existence remained unshaken by the letter. I
believed it to be nothing more nor less than a heartless
and stupid "hoax."

The striking of the hall-clock roused me from my medi-
tations. I counted the strokes,—midnight!

I rose to go up to my room. Everybody else in the
farm had retired to bed, as usual, more than an hour
since. The stillness in the house was breathless. I walked
softly, by instinct, as I crossed the room to look out at the

<94>

night. A lovely moonlight met my view: it was like the
moonlight on the fatal evening when Naomi had met
John Jago on the garden-walk.

My bedroom-candle was on the side-table: I had
just lit it. I was just leaving the room, when the door suddenly opened, and Naomi herself stood before me!

Recovering the first shock of her sudden appearance, I saw instantly, in her eager eyes, in her deadly-pale
cheeks, that something serious had happened. A large
cloak was thrown over her; a white handkerchief was tied
over her head. Her hair was in disorder: she had evidently
just risen in fear and in haste from her bed.

"What is it?" I asked, advancing to meet her.

She clung trembling with agitation to my arm.

"John Jago!" she whispered.

You will think my obstinacy invincible. I could
hardly believe it, even then!

"Where?" I asked.

"In the back yard," she replied, "under my bedroom-
window!"

The emergency was far too serious to allow of any
consideration for the small proprieties of every-day life.

"Let me see him!" I said.

"I am here to fetch you," she answered in her frank
and fearless way. "Come up stairs with me."

Her room was on the first floor of the house, and
was the only bedroom which looked out on the back yard.
On our way up the stairs she told me what had happened.

<95>

There was John Jago looking up at me.

"I was in bed," she said, "but not asleep, when I heard a pebble strike against the window-pane. I waited, wondering what it meant. Another pebble was thrown against the glass. So far, I was surprised, but not frightened. I got up, and ran to the window to look out. There was John Jago looking up at me in the moonlight!"

"Did he see you?"

"Yes. He said, 'Come down and speak to me! I have something serious to say to you!'"

"Did you answer him?"

"As soon as I could fetch my breath, I said, 'Wait a little,' and ran down stairs to you. What shall I do?"

"Let *me* see him, and I will tell you."

We entered her room. Keeping cautiously behind the window-curtain, I looked out.

There he was! His beard and mustache were shaved off: his hair was close cut. But there was no disguising his wild, brown eyes, or the peculiar movement of his spare, wiry figure, as he walked slowly to and fro in the moonlight, waiting for Naomi. For the moment, my own agitation almost overpowered me: I had so firmly disbelieved that John Jago was a living man!

"What shall I do?" Naomi repeated.

"Is the door of the dairy open?" I asked.

"No; but the door of the tool-house, round the corner, is not locked."

"Very good. Show yourself at the window, and say to him, 'I am coming directly.'"

<97>

The brave girl obeyed me without a moment's hesitation.

There had been no doubt about his eyes and his gait: there was no doubt now about his voice, as he answered softly from below,—

"All right!"

"Keep him talking to you where he is now," I said to Naomi, "until I have time to get round by the other way to the tool-house. Then pretend to be fearful of discovery at the dairy; and bring him round the corner, so that I can hear him behind the door."

We left the house together, and separated silently. Naomi followed my instructions with a woman's quick intelligence where stratagems are concerned. I had hardly been a minute in the tool-house before I heard him speaking to Naomi on the other side of the door.

The first words which I caught distinctly related to his motive for secretly leaving the farm. Mortified pride—doubly mortified by Naomi's contemptuous refusal, and by the personal indignity offered to him by Ambrose—was at the bottom of his conduct in absenting himself from Morwick. He owned that he had seen the advertisement, and that it had actually encouraged him to keep in hiding!

"After being laughed at and insulted and denied, I was glad," said the miserable wretch, "to see that some of you had serious reason to wish me back again. It rests with you, Miss Naomi, to keep me here, and to persuade me to save Ambrose by showing myself and owning to my name."

"What do you mean?" I heard Naomi ask sternly.

He lowered his voice; but I could still hear him.

"Promise you will marry me," he said, "and I will go before the magistrate to-morrow, and show him that I am a living man."

"Suppose I refuse?"

"In that case you will lose me again, and none of you will find me till Ambrose is hanged."

"Are you villain enough, John Jago, to mean what you say?" asked the girl, raising her voice.

"If you attempt to give the alarm," he answered, "as true as God's above us, you will feel my hand on your throat! It's my turn now, miss; and I am not to be trifled with. Will you have me for your husband,—yes or no?"

"No!" she answered loudly and firmly.

I burst open the door, and seized him as he lifted his hand on her. He had not suffered from the nervous derangement which had weakened me, and he was the stronger man of the two. Naomi saved my life. She struck up his pistol as he pulled it out of his pocket with his free hand and presented it at my head. The bullet was fired into the air. I tripped up his heels at the same moment. The report of the pistol had alarmed the house. We two together kept him on the ground until help arrived.

─ CHAPTER XII ─

The End of It

John Jago was brought before the magistrate, and John Jago was identified the next day.

The lives of Ambrose and Silas were, of course, no longer in peril, so far as human justice was concerned. But there were legal delays to be encountered, and legal formalities to be observed, before the brothers could be released from prison in the characters of innocent men.

During the interval which thus elapsed, certain events happened which may be briefly mentioned here before I close my narrative.

Mr. Meadowcroft the elder, broken by the suffering which he had gone through, died suddenly of a rheumatic affection of the heart. A codicil attached to his will abundantly justified what Naomi had told me of Miss Meadowcroft's influence over her father, and of the end she had in view in exercising it. A life-income only was left to Mr. Meadowcroft's sons. The freehold of the farm was bequeathed to his daughter, with the testator's rec-

<100>

ommendation added, that she should marry his "best and dearest friend, Mr. John Jago."

Armed with the power of the will, the heiress of Morwick sent an insolent message to Naomi, requesting her no longer to consider herself one of the inmates at the farm. Miss Meadowcroft, it should be here added, positively refused to believe that John Jago had ever asked Naomi to be his wife, or had ever threatened her, as I had heard him threaten her, if she refused. She accused me, as she accused Naomi, of trying meanly to injure John Jago in her estimation, out of hatred towards "that much-injured man;" and she sent to me, as she had sent to Naomi, a formal notice to leave the house.

We two banished ones met the same day in the hall, with our travelling-bags in our hands.

"We are turned out together, friend Lefrank," said Naomi with her quaintly comical smile. "You will go back to England, I guess; and I must make my own living in my own country. Women can get employment in the States if they have a friend to speak for them. Where shall I find somebody who can give me a place?"

I saw my way to saying the right word at the right moment.

"I have got a place to offer you," I replied. She suspected nothing, so far.

"That's lucky, sir," was all she said. "Is it in a telegraph-office, or in a dry-goods store?"

I astonished my little American friend by taking her then and there in my arms, and giving her my first kiss.

"The office is by my fireside," I said; "the salary is any thing in reason you like to ask me for; and the place, Naomi, if you have no objection to it, is the place of my wife."

I have no more to say, except that years have passed since I spoke those words, and that I am as fond of Naomi as ever.

Some months after our marriage, Mrs. Lefrank wrote to a friend at Narrabee for news of what was going on at the farm. The answer informed us that Ambrose and Silas had emigrated to New Zealand, and that Miss Meadowcroft was alone at Morwick Farm. John Jago had refused to marry her. John Jago had disappeared again, nobody knew where.

NOTE IN CONCLUSION.—The first idea of this little story was suggested to the author by a printed account of a trial which actually took place, early in the present century, in the United States. The published narrative of this strange case is entitled "The Trial, Confessions, and Conviction of Jesse and Stephen Boorn for the Murder of Russell Colvin, and the Return of the Man supposed to have been murdered. By Hon. Leonard Sargeant, Ex-Lieutenant-Governor of Vermont. (Manchester, Vermont, Journal Book and Job Office, 1873.)" It may not be amiss to add, for the benefit of incredulous readers, that all the "improbable events" in the story are matters of fact, taken from the printed narrative. Any thing which "looks like truth" is, in nine cases out of ten, the invention of the author.—W. C.

<102>

Wrongful Convictions

Rob Warden

The Boorn Case

The Dead Alive was inspired by events that occurred in Manchester, Vermont, between 1812 and 1820—a period telescoped into a few weeks in the novel.

John Jago's real-life counterpart was not an unprincipled farm overseer but a weak-minded farmhand named Russell Colvin, whose wife, Sally, was the sister of Stephen and Jesse Boorn, the real-life versions of Ambrose and Silas Meadowcroft.

The narrator, Philip Lefrank, and the Meadowcrofts' cousin, Naomi Colebrook, were inventions of Collins's bearing scant resemblance to anyone involved in the actual case.

When Sally married Russell in 1801, she was seventeen or eighteen years old and probably pregnant. Russell was about twenty-three and the prospective inheritor of his family's farm, which he had been managing, or rather mismanaging, since his father abandoned the family a year or

<105>

so earlier. Within a year of the wedding, the farm was in-solvent and the town of Manchester took it over, as the law allowed, to manage it in the interest of Russell's mother.

By the time Russell lost the farm, Sally had given birth to one child and was expecting another. She and Russell turned for help to her parents, Elizabeth and Barney Boorn. Like Isaac Meadowcroft in the novel, Barney was a relatively prosperous farmer. The Boorns agreed to take the Colvins in, in exchange for Russell working on the farm, alongside Stephen and Jesse.

Sally and Russell were still under the Boorn roof a decade later. And to the consternation of Stephen and Jesse, Sally had given birth not only to the additional child she was expecting in 1802 but to four others. With each arrival, the brothers became increasingly resentful that feeding the ballooning Colvin brood was draining the family resources.

Stephen, in particular, was not hesitant about vo-calizing his feelings. In the taverns he frequented, he took to calling his brother-in-law a laggard, a freeloader, and a Tory—a quintessential insult on the eve of the War of 1812. Given the animosity, it was hardly surpris-ing that Stephen and Russell would come to blows, as they purportedly did on May 10, 1812—the day Russell disappeared.

Neighbors soon became aware of Russell's absence but suspected nothing nefarious. He had disappeared before

<106>

without notice, once for nine months, and his wanderings were hardly surprising because the Colvins' marriage was not a model of love and contentment.

Sally had been known to absent herself from Manchester on occasion for suspected liaisons with a person or persons of the opposite sex. In fact, she had been away on May 10. Upon her return, five days later—according to her testimony seven years after the fact—she asked her eldest child, ten-year-old Lewis, where his father was.

"Gone to hell," Lewis answered.

If Sally had any indication of foul play, however, she did not betray her suspicion beyond the family. Of course, it would not have been in her interest to occasion an official investigation. If Russell had been murdered, the prime suspects would have been her brothers and perhaps her father, upon whom she and her children were dependent for sustenance.

When neighbors inquired about Russell, the Boorns' stock reply was simply that he had run away, perhaps to join the military. In light of Russell's proclivity for wandering and failure as a family provider, there was little reason initially for anyone to doubt that explanation. But as months passed with no sign of Russell, questions arose, owing to two family propensities—Sally's for promiscuity and Stephen's for talking too much.

In the summer of 1813, Sally gave birth to a little girl, her seventh child. This resulted in her expulsion from the Manchester Baptist Church—the birth having occurred more than a gestation period after Russell's disappearance. Church officials were discreet about the action, sparing the family disgrace. But for the Boorns, Sally's indiscretion meant another child to feed and clothe.

The strain on the family's resources might have been alleviated by support from the newborn's father. But that option was not pursued, perhaps because legal action would have entailed a public disclosure that the child had been born out of wedlock.

Two years later, however, public embarrassment was unavoidable when Sally gave birth to her eighth child. With reputational damage no longer an issue—it being obvious to the community that this child could not have been fathered by Russell—Sally consulted a lawyer about "swearing the child": identifying the father and legally compelling him to provide support.

Swearing the child, it turned out, would be problematic. The lawyer told Sally that since she was lawfully married, the law presumed her husband to be the father. It mattered not that Russell had been gone for three years. To pursue her paramour for support, the lawyer advised, Sally would have to establish that Russell was dead—and had been at the time of the child's conception.

When Sally explained the situation to her family, Stephen reportedly responded incredulously that he knew for a fact that Russell was dead. Such a statement would have had no consequence had it remained in the family, but Stephen could not resist grousing publicly about what seemed to him absurd. (Had Wilkie Collins's friend Charles Dickens written *The Dead Alive,* Ambrose Meadowcroft might have said, "If the law says that, the law is an ass.")

Stephen's indiscretion naturally caused people to wonder how he could be so sure Russell was dead. Talk in the taverns and tabernacles of the town turned to the possibility that one or more of the Boorns—Stephen, Jesse, Barney—had had something to do with their annoying in-law's disappearance.

Amid such chatter, one of the Boorns' neighbors suddenly recalled having seen Stephen and Jesse quarreling with Russell on May 10, 1812—and no one in Manchester had seen Russell since. The neighbor who claimed to have witnessed the quarrel was Thomas Johnson, who would play a pivotal—and, it seems, ignoble—role in the ensuing drama.

Another neighbor recalled that not long before Russell vanished, Stephen had wondered out loud if there might be a way to prevent Sally and Russell from having sex and issuing offspring. When the neighbor opined that there was no way—save a rather obvious one—Stephen allegedly vowed to put a stop to their profligate behavior somehow. And a cousin of the Boorns quoted Stephen as having said, in about April 1812, that he would relish

<109>

kicking Sally and Russell into hell, even if he burnt his legs off in the process.

In March 1815, a fire of mysterious origin destroyed a sheep barn near the spot where Stephen and Russell were said to have fought the day the latter disappeared. Four months before the fire, Barney Boorn had sold the parcel of land on which the barn stood to Thomas Johnson, the owner of adjacent property. As the embers cooled, neighbors speculated that the fire was somehow related to Russell's disappearance.

A few days later, Thomas Johnson's children, or so Johnson reported, found a "very moldy and rotten" black hat on the former Boorn property. The hat was similar to one Russell had been known to have owned. For Colvin's sister, Clarissa Ferguson, the alleged discovery was proof positive that something untoward had become of her brother. Russell, she asserted, would not have been one to go about the country unsuitably hatted.

Thus the tide of public opinion turned—based on rumor and innuendo stemming from Stephen's barroom blabbering, others' recollections of events and conversations that had occurred three years earlier, a mysterious fire, and an old hat—and a chorus arose demanding action. As Philip Lefrank observed in the novel, "Public opinion declares itself in America, without the slightest reserve, or the slightest care for consequences."

One consequence was to prompt Stephen to forsake

<*110*>

Manchester in early 1817. His father had given him most of the proceeds from the sale of the parcel of land to Thomas Johnson, and he had bought a small farm.

When a freeze struck in the late spring of 1816, Stephen fell on hard times. Now married and the father of three, he moved his family two hundred miles to Denmark, New York—a move no doubt motivated by a desire to escape the suspicion that he had been instrumental in bringing on himself.

In March 1819, after two years in New York, Stephen returned to Manchester for a family visit. Finding rumors still rampant that he had slain Russell, he falsely asserted to assorted acquaintances that he and Jesse had been away from the farm on May 10, 1812. In an ill-advised effort to support the alibi, Elizabeth and Barney Boorn repeated the falsehood. Again, the family propensity for loose talk would make matters worse.

Although the Boorns did not yet appear to be in legal jeopardy, that situation was about to change as a result of what would be perceived in some quarters as supernatural intervention—the appearance of Russell Colvin's ghost. The specter purportedly appeared not to the Methodist preacher conjured up by Wilkie Collins but to Amos Boorn, a younger brother of Barney and an uncle of Stephen and Jesse.

Amos claimed that the ghost had come to him three

times in dreams, confirming each time, as was now widely assumed, that his life had ended violently. Although the ghost apparently did not identify his killer or killers, he was said to have led the slumbering Amos to the place of his interment—not the lime kiln of the novel but an abandoned root cellar (a hole in which potatoes were stowed below the frost line) on the parcel of land that Barney had sold to Thomas Johnson in 1814.

Amos was, in the words of the Reverend Lemuel Haynes, pastor of the Congregationalist church, "a gentleman of respectability, whose character was unimpeachable." Consequently, his story was widely accepted.

Russell's ghost, to quote Samuel Putnam Waldo, a Hartford attorney who wrote an account of the case in 1820, "seemed to have had, if possible, a more serious effect upon the minds of the people than that of the King of Denmark upon Hamlet."

As Philip Lefrank observed in *The Dead Alive*, "the public voice insisted on the necessity of a search for the mortal remains" of the presumed victim.

On April 27, 1819, a court of inquiry was convened to investigate the case. It was led by the town clerk, Joel Pratt, and the town elected grand juror, Truman Hill.

Jesse Boorn was arrested, as Stephen would have been had he not been a hard three days' distance away in New York.

The function of the court of inquiry was similar in

<112>

some ways to that of a modern police detective bureau, although dissimilar in other ways. It searched for evidence in the manner of a latter-day field investigation but also took sworn testimony in public proceedings.

The first ostensible action of the court was to exclude spectral evidence—testimony regarding Russell's ghost. Practically that meant that Amos Boorn would not testify, although his story had prompted the proceedings and would haunt them throughout.

Amos, moreover, was present at the public sessions and permitted to ask questions. He also was assigned to lead the excavation of the abandoned root cellar on April 28. Although no human remains were found, the exercise turned up a penknife, a jackknife, and what looked like a button from a coat.

Richard Skinner, a prominent Manchester lawyer and former congressman, was assigned to accompany Joel Pratt to show the potential items of evidence to Sally Colvin, who identified them as having been Russell's.

As sensational as Sally's claim was, it fell short of proving that a murder had occurred. And when nothing else inculpatory was forthcoming, Pratt and Hill were on the verge of ending the inquiry after four days of proceedings. However, Thomas Johnson, who claimed to have seen Stephen and Jesse quarreling with Russell seven years earlier, asked to take a crack at eliciting a confession.

After all that had gone before, it seemed highly un-

<113>

likely that Jesse would suddenly abandon his staunch insistence that he knew nothing of Russell's fate. Nonetheless, the court of inquiry authorized Johnson to speak to Jesse in his cell the evening of May 1, 1819. At some point, Truman Hill took over the questioning and emerged to announce a major breakthrough: Jesse had implicated Stephen in the murder of Russell Colvin.

Jesse had not witnessed the crime but claimed that Stephen had confided, during his recent visit to Manchester, that in 1812 he had struck Russell and "laid him aside, where no one would find him." Until Stephen said that, Jesse claimed he had not suspected that Russell had been murdered. Upon reflection after Stephen's return to Denmark, Jesse said he had figured out approximately where Stephen had buried the body.

While Jesse's statement did not substantively resemble that of Silas Meadowcroft accusing Ambrose of murdering John Jago, the motives may well have been the same: Jesse may have, to quote Naomi Colebrook, "lied away his brother's life to save himself."

According to John S. Pettibone, a justice of the peace briefly involved in the case, Jesse made his statement under duress, having been threatened with execution—"You are a gone goose"—unless he gave a full description of how Stephen murdered Russell.

Jesse's description of Russell's possible grave site prompted a resumption of the search at daybreak on Sunday, May 2.

The search turned up nothing, but late in the day a boy came forward to report that he had found something of possible interest. The previous day, said the boy, he had been walking with his dog along the Battenkill River, which abutted the Boorn farm, when the dog suddenly ran to a hollow stump, barking furiously. Inside or beneath the stump, the boy found several charred bones.

Joel Pratt and Amos Boorn collected the bones, which, of course, were presumed to be the theretofore elusive evidence of murder—a presumption supported a few days later by four local physicians who examined the bones and pronounced them human.

The court of inquiry, meanwhile, questioned Lewis Colvin. He testified that on May 10, 1812, he had been working with his father, who began acting strangely. Lewis said he became frightened and ran home. But as the questioning continued, he modified the story, saying he had seen his father and uncle fight—presumably resulting in his father's death.

In light of the physicians' opinions and Lewis's claim that there had been a fight, a warrant was issued for Stephen's arrest. A posse embarked for New York and returned with Stephen in chains on May 15.

The next day, a Sunday, Elizabeth Boorn was expelled from the Manchester Baptist Church for her clumsy attempt to corroborate the alibi Stephen had fabricated for May 10, 1812.

Barney Boorn, who had been equally culpable in

corroborating the alibi, was not subject to the church's sanction because he was not a member. But something more onerous was in store for him—he was about to be arrested as a possible accessory to murder.

When the court of inquiry resumed its public proceedings with three suspects in custody, one of the physicians who had examined the burnt bones announced that he had been hasty in his initial conclusion. After comparing the bones to a human skeleton, he had changed his opinion. He was now certain that they were not human after all.

The other three physicians defended their initial contention but agreed that further study was advisable. To that end, they exhumed a recently amputated human leg for comparison. Once that was done, the three concurred with their colleague that the bones definitely were of nonhuman origin.

With the case again close to disintegrating, the inquiry was on the verge of ending when Silas Merrill, an accused perjurer who shared a cell with Jesse Boorn, came forward to claim that his cell mate had confessed.

According to Merrill, Jesse awakened in great fright in the middle of the night and proclaimed that something had come into the cell—implicitly, Russell's ghost—and was at that moment on the bed beside him.

Jesse proceeded to relate, according to Merrill, that

<116>

on May 10, 1812, he, Stephen, and Russell had been working in the field where Thomas Johnson supposedly saw them arguing. The argument escalated into violence and, as Lewis Colvin testified, there had been a fight.

Stephen knocked Russell to the ground. Barney then happened along and, seeing that Russell was still alive, cut his throat with a penknife. They buried Russell in the root cellar, as Russell's ghost had indicated to Amos Boorn. Later, fearing that the remains might be discovered, they moved them to the sheep barn. Then, when fire destroyed the barn, they moved the remains again—this time to the stump where the boy and the dog found them.

Aside from Merrill's intrinsic credibility issue, he being an accused perjurer, there was a more serious problem with his story—namely that it flew in the face of the consensus of the medical men of Manchester that the bones in question were nonhuman.

But that was a problem that the court of inquiry could and would solve—by ignoring it.

Merrill's description of Jesse's alleged implication of Barney and Stephen in the purported murder was, of course, hearsay and therefore legally useless against them. Since there was no other evidence linking Barney to the crime, the charges against him were dismissed by Justice of the Peace John Pettibone.

But since there was other evidence against Ste-

<117>

phen—principally Lewis Colvin's contention that he had witnessed an argument that came to blows in 1812—the court of inquiry held Stephen for further investigation, along with Jesse, who, if Merrill was to be believed, had inculpated himself.

Viewed in the light most damaging to the brothers, the evidence that a crime had been committed remained largely circumstantial and otherwise weak and contradictory. Despite rampant prejudice among the populace against the Boorns, moreover, there was a possibility that a jury might take seriously its oath to require proof of guilt beyond a reasonable doubt—a problematic prospect for a prosecution.

What was needed was a confession from Stephen—and the court of inquiry set about obtaining one.

While the tactics employed were not gentle, they were more psychological than physical.

The strategy—as two of Stephen's interrogators would unabashedly acknowledge—was to persuade him that his only hope of escaping the noose was to confess.

On August 27, 1819, Stephen succumbed to fear and wrote a detailed confession (see "Stephen Boorn's Written Confession").

The document was ungrammatical and otherwise awkward but artfully self-serving, portraying Russell's death as manslaughter—a crime for which one might be let off with a whipping—and absolving Barney and Jesse of any role in the crime.

According to the confession, Russell and Lewis were working in the field where the crime was assumed to have occurred on May 10, 1812. Stephen came along and got into an argument with Russell, who picked up a birch tree limb and struck Stephen with it. Thereupon Stephen grabbed the limb and clubbed Russell to the ground.

The confession continued that Lewis saw the fight but did not realize his father was mortally wounded. Later, when the boy asked if his father had been killed, Stephen said no, that he had just gone away, and told Lewis to say nothing about the fight. After putting Russell's body in the abandoned root cellar, Stephen wrote, he "went home crying."

For a reason not explained, Stephen moved the remains a year or two later to the sheep barn. Then, after the 1815 fire, he moved them again. This time he threw the larger bones into the Battenkill River and, for another unexplained reason, hid some of the smaller ones in the hollow stump. Stephen's account of his final disposition of the remains was thus consistent with the account Merrill attributed to Jesse, and it therefore conflicted irreconcilably with the medical evidence.

Within days, Stephen recanted, proclaiming that he had fabricated the confession in the belief that confess-

<119>

ing was the only way he could save his life. But the court of inquiry found the recantation unpersuasive and, still untroubled by the contradictory medical evidence, recommended that both Stephen and his brother be prosecuted for murder.

State's Attorney Calvin Sheldon presented the case to the regular grand jury of Bennington County on September 26, 1819, relying on a single witness—Silas Merrill.

Sheldon apparently chose not to introduce Stephen's confession because it would have undermined the theory that the brothers acted in concert. Merrill's dubious tale of Jesse's midnight confession was all Sheldon needed.

The grand jury returned a true bill charging the brothers—"not having the fear of God before their eyes, but being moved and seduced by the instigation of the devil"—with the murder of Russell Colvin.

Early-nineteenth-century criminal trial procedures in Vermont differed strikingly from procedures that evolved in ensuing decades.

One difference was that capital cases were presided over by the three-member state Supreme Court, rather than a single lower court judge. Since there was no higher court, there was no right to appeal within the judiciary, although verdicts and sentences were subject to review by the Vermont General Assembly.

<120>

Another difference was that evidentiary issues were decided not by the court but by the jury—a procedure that made the jury privy to information that was irrelevant to its ultimate determination of guilt or innocence.

A third difference was that defendants were not allowed to testify, the theory being that their incentive to lie was so great that whatever they might say would be unworthy of credence.

The Vermont Supreme Court convened in Manchester on October 27, 1819, to try the Boorn case, with Chief Judge Dudley Chase, a former United States senator from Vermont, presiding. Because the crowd was larger than the local courthouse could accommodate, the judges moved the trial across the street to the Congregational church, which had a capacity of several hundred but nonetheless overflowed throughout the five-day trial.

The Boorns were represented by three lawyers, Richard Skinner, Leonard Sargeant, and Daniel Wellman. Despite their clients' potentially conflicting defenses, the defense team represented them jointly—a precarious situation that would not be tolerated by modern courts. Moreover, two of the defense lawyers, Skinner and Wellman, became trial witnesses—which also would be verboten today.

After entering pleas of not guilty on behalf of the Boorns, the defense moved to sever the trials, but the motion was summarily denied. Then came jury selection.

<121>

Twenty-nine prospective jurors were examined. Eleven were dismissed for cause and each side exercised three peremptory challenges. That left twelve qualified jurors, who were sworn and seated.

Calvin Sheldon's first witness was none other than the lead defense counsel, Richard Skinner, who testified that Sally Colvin had identified the knives and the button recovered from the root cellar as Russell's. Sheldon easily could have elicited the same facts by calling Joel Pratt, who had been with Skinner when Sally was shown the items, but the effect would not have been the same.

Next Sheldon called Amos Boorn, who related that he had been present for the recovery of the items in question. Again, Sheldon could have documented the discovery with other witnesses, but Amos's appearance on the stand was a pointed reminder to the jury that the defendants' own uncle had all but accused them of Russell's murder.

Thomas Johnson was called to recount his claim that he had seen Stephen and Russell arguing the day the latter vanished, and Lewis Colvin, now seventeen, described the supposed fight that ensued. Sheldon also called Eunice and Daniel Baldwin, who belatedly claimed that Stephen, in an unguarded moment in 1815, had let slip that he and Jesse had put Russell's body "where potatoes would not freeze"—implicitly, the root cellar.

When Sheldon sought to introduce Stephen's writ-

<122>

ten confession, Skinner strenuously objected on the ground that the circumstances under which it had been elicited rendered it unreliable.

In support of his position, Skinner called two witnesses who had been involved in Stephen's interrogation. The first was Truman Hill, who forthrightly acknowledged that he had repeatedly exhorted Stephen that confessing was "the only way to pardon or favor." The second was Samuel Raymond, who was even more candid. Not only had he exhorted Stephen to confess on the same ground but he also had heard Joel Pratt and Calvin Sheldon do so.

After hearing Hill and Raymond's testimony—which Sheldon made no effort to rebut—the jury had no choice, under instructions from the judges, but to hold Stephen's written confession inadmissible.

From a practical standpoint, however, the victory was hollow for the defense. The fact that Stephen had confessed had been indelibly etched in jurors' minds. Furthermore, the exclusion did not apply to Silas Merrill's account of Jesse's purported midnight declaration or to the testimony of another witness, who also claimed that Stephen had confessed.

The latter witness was William Farnsworth, one of Manchester's premier drunks, who frequently visited Stephen, a fellow imbiber, in jail. During a visit some two weeks after Stephen gave the written confession, according to Farnsworth, Stephen told him "he wished he had that paper back" but went on to acknowledge that he had killed Russell and "put the pieces of the bones under the stump."

Farnsworth's account—like Merrill's testimony and Stephen's confession—flew in the face of the medical evidence, but the contradiction was not apparent to the jury, which had received no anatomical evidence.

When the prosecution rested, Richard Skinner called four witnesses—Sally Colvin, her sister-in-law, Clarissa Ferguson, and two neighbors of the Boorns—to establish that Russell had a predilection for disappearing for extended periods.

Next, Skinner attacked Merrill's credibility—an endeavor that probably would have been more compelling had it not relied principally on the testimony of Daniel Wellman, a member of the defense team.

Wellman told the jury that, after he learned of Jesse's purported inculpatory statement, he went to the jail to speak with Merrill, whom he once represented. According to Wellman, Merrill admitted that he had concocted the story of the so-called midnight confession; it was implicit that the motive for the fabrication was to win the favor of the authorities.

Following Wellman to the stand was Cyrus Munson, one of the jailers, from whom Skinner elicited that Merrill had been confined in chains before he reported the alleged confession but afterward had been unchained

<124>

and also had been allowed to leave the jail to attend to personal business.

Skinner inexplicably did not play the ace he was holding: he failed to call any of the physicians who had unanimously agreed that the bones recovered from the stump were not human.

The omission was of such magnitude that it is hard to imagine that it was only an oversight. Perhaps, in the face of the overwhelming public opinion against the Boorns, the physicians were reluctant to help them. And perhaps the Boorns' lawyers, in turn, chose not to offend the physicians by compelling them to testify.

If so, the extension of professional courtesy from the legal to the medical profession, in violation of the ethical principles of both, left the defendants in jeopardy of conviction and execution for a crime they did not commit.

And given the meager evidence adduced by the defense, it was anything but irrational for the jurors to unanimously conclude—as they would within an hour after the lawyers' summations and the judges' instructions on October 31, 1819—that the Boorn brothers were guilty as charged.

The convictions carried automatic death sentences.

Leonard Sargeant, the junior member of the defense team, promptly left for Montpelier to seek clemency. Relief would require the concurrence of a majority of mem-

<125>

bers of the Vermont General Assembly, then a unicameral body, and Governor Jonas Galusha.

After requesting and receiving Judge Chase's trial notes, the General Assembly took up the case on November 15, 1819, voting 104 to 33 to reduce Jesse's sentence to life at hard labor but denying Stephen relief by a vote of 97 to 43. Later that day, Governor Galusha concurred.

Stephen's hanging was scheduled for January 28, 1820.

Governor Galusha personally delivered the news to Stephen on November 17, 1819.

The condemned man was despondent, but soon regained his composure.

By the time Sargeant visited after Galusha left, Stephen had come up with an idea that years later would incorrectly be credited with saving his life—placing a newspaper advertisement seeking to locate Colvin.

Sargeant relayed the idea to Skinner, who scoffed. But seeing no harm in humoring a man in a seemingly hopeless situation, Skinner wrote a notice, which Sargeant inserted into the most prominent publication in the vicinity, the *Rutland Herald*, on November 30, 1819:

> MURDER.—Printers of newspapers throughout the United States are desired to publish that Stephen Boorn, of Manchester, in Vermont, is sentenced to be executed for the murder of Russell Colvin, who has

been absent about seven years. Any person who can give information of said Colvin may save the life of the innocent by making immediate communication. Colvin is about five feet five inches high, light complexion, light coloured hair, blue eyes, about forty years of age.

Sargeant—in a pamphlet that was published in 1873 and that inspired the Wilkie Collins novel published the following year—credited the advertisement with bringing about Colvin's return.

But that was a myth, which Collins would perpetuate, as would Edwin M. Borchard, a Yale law professor and former librarian of Congress, in a seminal study of wrongful convictions published in 1932.

Borchard entitled his account of the case "A Corpse Answers an Advertisement."

What actually happened was recounted by Gerald W. McFarland, a professor of history at the University of Massachusetts, who rigorously researched the case in the late 1980s.

Colvin's reappearance in Manchester, McFarland discovered, had nothing to do with the advertisement that appeared in the *Rutland Herald*. Rather, Colvin emerged as a result of an anonymous letter that was published five days earlier in the *Albany Gazette and Daily Advertiser* and was reprinted on November 26 by the *New York Evening Post*.

THE

TRIAL, CONFESSIONS

AND CONVICTION

OF

JESSE AND STEPHEN BOORN

FOR THE MURDER OF

RUSSELL COLVIN,

AND

THE RETURN OF THE MAN SUPPOSED TO HAVE
BEEN MURDERED.

By Hon. LEONARD SARGEANT.

Ex-Lieut Governor of Vermont.

————◄•●•►————

MANCHESTER, VT.:
JOURNAL BOOK AND JOB OFFICE.
1873.

Leonard Sargeant's 1873 pamphlet on which Wilkie Collins based
The Dead Alive

The letter marveled that "a most striking example of divine agency" had brought two killers to justice. It mentioned Russell Colvin, speculating that his fate would have remained forever unknown had his ghost not appeared to reveal "that he had been murdered by two persons whom he named"—a revelation that prompted a search leading to the discovery of "a human skeleton" and the arrest of the killers the ghost had identified.

That the letter played fast and loose with the facts was of no import. What mattered was that it was read aloud in a public room of a New York City hotel in the presence of Tabor Chadwick, a Methodist minister from Shrewsbury, New Jersey, and James Whelpley, a New York tavern keeper and native of Manchester.

Upon hearing the name Russell Colvin, Chadwick proclaimed that he knew a man who called himself that— and who, for the last several years, had been working as a farmhand in Dover, New Jersey, for William Polhemus, Chadwick's brother-in-law.

Whelpley, who had had a passing acquaintance with Colvin, soon set off for Dover. There he located Polhemus, who confirmed that a man identifying himself as Colvin had shown up several years earlier. Although the man seemed not quite right in the head, Polhemus had found him likable and given him a job with room and board. At the moment, said Polhemus, the man was off working the fields but Whelpley was welcome to await his return.

<129>

When the man came in that evening, Whelpley greeted him by name. At first, the man denied being Colvin, but after some prodding allowed that he once had been Colvin but now was someone else. As the conversation continued, Colvin revealed memories of Manchester, leaving no doubt in Whelpley's mind that he had found the presumed dead man alive.

Colvin, however, was reluctant to entertain Whelpley's suggestion that they return together to Manchester.

Time being of the essence—this according to an 1820 account by the Reverend Lemuel Haynes—Whelpley enlisted a young woman to entice Colvin to accompany her to New York City. If Haynes's account is to be believed, Colvin eagerly accepted the invitation. When they arrived in the city, according to plan, the woman deserted him. Whelpley then told Colvin that because British warships were offshore, they would be well advised to take a circuitous route back to New Jersey. With this subterfuge, Whelpley coaxed Colvin onto a stagecoach bound for Manchester.

As implausible as this scenario might seem, it was widely accepted as gospel at the time, owing no doubt to the stature of the Reverend Haynes, who was respected and renowned throughout New England for sermons that moved the faithful to tears.

In any case, the journey itself was well documented. Newspapers reported the passing of Colvin and Whelpley through Albany on December 21, 1819, and when the

<130>

pair reached Bennington the next day, a rider was dispatched to Manchester to spread the word that they were en route.

A crowd gathered in front of Captain Black's Tavern in Manchester to greet Colvin and Whelpley upon their arrival at sunset on December 22. Among the crowd were several men and women whom Colvin addressed by name—thereby establishing to the satisfaction of all that reports of his demise had been greatly exaggerated.

Stephen was brought from the jail to Captain Black's, and Russell asked in seeming astonishment why he was in chains.

"Because they say I murdered you," Stephen replied.

A celebration ensued, continuing into the night and resuming the next morning, the public mood having come full circle.

Quoth Sargeant, "The most extravagant expressions of joy were indulged in by the people who, at last convinced of their error, were only too glad to make reparation."

Russell's reappearance presented a perplexing procedural problem for the authorities. The question was not what the result should be but rather how to achieve it.

Pending official exoneration, Stephen was released on his own recognizance by the Manchester authorities. But they could not release Jesse because he had been moved the previous month to begin his life at hard labor at the state penitentiary in Windsor, Vermont.

Fortuitously, the Vermont Supreme Court, which traveled a circuit like the lower courts of the day, was scheduled to convene in Bennington on January 18, 1820.

The night before the session, Leonard Sargeant met with the judges at the inn where they were staying. According to Sargeant's 1873 account, one of the judges asked him, "Well, Brother Sargeant, what are you going to do about this? I suppose you have some plan concocted?"

He did indeed.

The plan—which was without precedent but in which the prosecutor, Calvin Sheldon, concurred—was to ask for a new trial based on newly discovered evidence.

The next day, the Supreme Court summarily granted the motion, whereupon Sheldon stepped forward and dropped the charges.

The Boorn brothers thus became the first of eleven defendants known to have been convicted in the United States of murdering victims who turned out not to have been dead (see "Other Dead Alive Cases").

The exoneration of the Boorns received prominent play in newspapers throughout New England. In Vermont, the reporting was reasonably accurate, but elsewhere the facts seldom stood in the way making a good story better.

One error that frequently made it into print was

<132>

that the Boorns' wrongful convictions had rested upon spectral evidence. Although the prosecution had made no attempt to introduce such evidence, that reality escaped the attention of the popular press. The misimpression prompted a plethora of editorials demanding an evidentiary reform that in fact had been in place since the Salem witchcraft trials of 1692.

Commentators learned in the law focused on correcting the misinformation, while ignoring the actual problems that led to the wrongful convictions—particularly jailhouse snitch testimony and false confessions.

Nor did Wilkie Collins see the case as more than a regrettable and freakish anomaly in an otherwise functioning criminal justice system. When he wrote *The Dead Alive* in 1873, of course, he could not appreciate the prevalence of the errors that led to the miscarriage of justice in Boorn case.

But by the early twenty-first century, 235 men and women had been exonerated after having been condemned to die in the United States. The wrongful condemnations were the result of various factors, but fifty-nine involved false admissions and seventy-nine testimony by in-custody informants, known in the vernacular as snitches, or by other witnesses with incentives to lie, such as the actual culprits (see "Wrongful Convictions in U.S. Capital Cases").

Had Collins been aware of the extent of the problem, *The Dead Alive* might have been more didactic,

<133>

given that Collins, by all accounts, was never hesitant to champion a cause.

While Silas and the jilted Ambrose Meadowcroft sailed off to New Zealand to live out their years, their real-life counterparts went to Ohio.

In January 1820, Russell Colvin disappeared again. As with John Jago in the novel, nobody knew where.

Sally Colvin married a man named Daniel Holmes and moved to Shaftsbury, Vermont, where she died in 1864.

Richard Skinner went on to be elected governor of Vermont, serving from 1820 to 1823, and then served as a judge of the Vermont Supreme Court until he was killed in a carriage accident in 1833.

Leonard Sargeant held various public offices, including Bennington County state's attorney, probate judge, state representative, and, finally, lieutenant governor.

After retiring from public life, Sargeant wrote his pamphlet on the Boorn case, which Collins ran across on a book tour of upstate New York in September 1873.

In Ohio, according to Gerald McFarland, Stephen and Jesse Boorn each acquired a modest farm near the west branch of the Cuyahoga River.

Hundreds of New Englanders, including several from the Manchester vicinity, had been drawn to Ohio

<134>

by the lure of cheap land. But by the time the Boorns arrived most of the better land had been taken. Consequently, their agricultural ventures were only marginally successful, although they were generally regarded, at least initially, as hardworking and respectable.

Jesse tired of dirt farming and at some point turned to something more lucrative—counterfeiting. In 1860, a deputy U.S. marshal working undercover infiltrated the venture and gathered evidence leading to Jesse's arrest. At his trial, according to McFarland, Jesse feigned "feebleness and palsy" in an effort to garner sympathy. He nonetheless was convicted and on August 1, 1860, sentenced to five years in the Ohio State Penitentiary at Columbus.

Jesse's prison admission record listed his age as seventy-five, although he was only sixty-seven or sixty-eight. And according to the record, he stood five five, had sunken hazel eyes, gray hair, an oval face, a dark complexion, and was missing one lower front tooth.

About the time Jesse got into trouble, Stephen moved to Eaton Rapids, Michigan, where he lived in obscurity until his death on March 7, 1869. His wife, Polly, either did not accompany him to Michigan or after his death returned to Ohio, where she died in 1878.

The deputy U.S. marshal who developed the 1860 counterfeiting case against Jesse Boorn told newspaper reporters an intriguing but seemingly far-fetched tale, suggesting that the man who showed up in Manchester

<135>

forty years before purporting to be Colvin had been an imposter.

The marshal, who was never officially identified but whom Gerald McFarland believes was H. M. Hackett of Ravenna, Ohio, claimed he asked Jesse if he had ever been involved in crimes other than counterfeiting.

Yes, Jesse answered, he and his brother had murdered their brother-in-law, been tried, and sentenced to hang. But after ascending the scaffold and having nooses placed around their necks, they saved themselves by arranging to have "a man from New Jersey who bore a striking resemblance to the deceased" show up just in time to stop the execution.

The most likely explanation of the genesis of such a seemingly preposterous tale is that Jesse concocted it to impress a man he presumed to be a confederate. The embellishments that were contrary to the facts would lend credence to that explanation. Less likely is the possibility that Jesse related either an accurate or embellished version of the actual story to the deputy marshal, who then took dramatic license with some of the facts, including the part about the man being an imposter.

Another possibility is that, despite the disinformation about the condemned men having the ropes around their necks, the man was a fake—a theory McFarland explored in a book about the case. Although McFarland's title—*The Counterfeit Man*—suggested that he endorsed the imposter notion, his account was nonjudgmental.

<136>

When McFarland's book was published in 1990, the idea that Colvin might have been a phony probably seemed more plausible than it would seem today. The French film *Le Retour de Martin Guerre*—the story of how an imposter named Arnaud du Tilh deluded the residents of Artigat for three years in the late 1550s—recently had enjoyed a good run in the United States. And the phenomenon of false confessions, absent torture, was not generally understood until DNA exposed its ubiquity in the last decade of the twentieth century.

What renders the imposter idea implausible, however, is the complexity and magnitude of the conspiracy that would have been necessary to stage such a deception. Not only would the plot have required the complicity of Stephen Boorn, Leonard Sargeant, and James Whelpley, but they would have had to find a Colvin look-alike capable of a performance worthy of an Academy Award.

Could the Boorns' wrongful convictions occur today?

Probably not—only because DNA testing would establish that the skeletal remains from the stump were not human.

But the other major problems that led to the wrongful convictions have not been adequately addressed by advances in the law or science.

Consider, first, false confessions. The notion that anyone of sound mind would freely confess to a crime he

<137>

or she did not commit, especially one punishable by death, seems counterintuitive, to say the least. Yet Stephen Boorn—and scores of murder suspects after him— did just that, veritably in the shadow of the gallows.

The Boorn case sheds light on the phenomenon.

When Jesse attributed the murder to Stephen, the evidence that the crime had occurred appeared strong. There was no question that Russell had disappeared, and the brothers' well-known dislike for him seemed motive enough for murder. What Jesse probably believed to be human remains had been found.

The evidence of guilt seemed stronger yet when Stephen was confronted with it. His own brother had blamed him for the purported crime. Moreover, Silas Merrill had neatly tied many of the presumed facts together—explaining the migration of the bones from the cellar hole to the barn to the stump.

It was hardly irrational, albeit ill advised, for Stephen to state that he had killed Colvin but had done so in self-defense—a fabrication minimizing his culpability in the hope of avoiding a death sentence.

Hope as one might that the U.S. Supreme Court's 1966 *Miranda* decision requiring police to inform suspects of their right to remain silent would prevent such grievous mistakes today, empirical scholarship on the decision indicates that it has had negligible impact on the ability of the police to elicit confessions.

Consider, next, snitches, whose history in the Anglo-American criminal justice system is long, inglorious, and—despite their notorious unreliability—continuing to unfold.

It would be a felony for a defense lawyer to promise a prospective witness anything of value in exchange for testimony. Yet, with impunity, prosecutors routinely promise and deliver something of greater value than anything a criminally inclined defense lawyer possibly could promise—freedom from punishment for a serious offense.

The practice is tantamount to bribery, as a panel of the U.S. Court of Appeals for the Tenth Circuit held in 1998 in a case called *U.S. v. Singleton*—only to be reversed by the full Tenth Circuit. The full court did not even attempt to rebut the obvious fact that rewarding snitches with leniency was basically bribery. Rather, said the court, the time-honored practice had "acquired stature akin to the special privilege of kings."

In sum, it is fair to say, two of the systemic problems that led to the wrongful convictions of the Boorns—false confessions and snitches—have stubbornly persisted into the twenty-first century.

But would not the modern application of the corpus delicti rule prevent a prosecution without a body?

Contrary to popular lore, the production of a body

<*139*>

is not necessarily a prerequisite to a murder prosecution. The corpus delicti rule merely bars convictions based on confessions without independent proof that a crime occurred, while the vast majority of murder confessions occur in cases in which the crime is an indisputable fact and the only question is who committed it.

Because corpus delicti does nothing to prevent convictions based on confessions to actual murders, its primary effect is not to protect the wrongfully accused who falsely confess but rather to protect the criminal justice system from the sort of embarrassment that would attend a modern "dead alive" case.

Public enthusiasm for executions was never great in Vermont, and the exoneration of the Boorns dampened it further.

The first execution under color of law there was that of a Tory named David Redding, who was convicted of treason in 1778, his underlying crime being the theft of horses for the British army from the U.S. government.

Two thorny technicalities were overlooked in the case—one being that the crime had occurred not in Vermont but in New York, the other that Vermont was not yet a state and thus had no authority to prosecute federal crimes.

But Redding successfully appealed on the ground

that juries, according to Blackstone, were supposed to have twelve members. A mob thereupon mobilized to lynch Redding, but Ethan Allen, the renowned leader of the Green Mountain Boys, stepped forward to quell the anger. The mob dispersed—a victory for civil authority over anarchy, perhaps, although one of little benefit to Redding, who immediately was retried before a venire of twelve and hanged.

From Vermont's admission to the union in 1791 until the Boorn exoneration twenty-nine years later, there were three more executions. All were for murder, although the law—carried over from the Republic of Vermont—extended the death penalty to, inter alia, rape, burglary, arson, sodomy, bestiality, and blasphemy.

When there had not been another execution by 1838, Governor Silas Jenison called for abolishing the death penalty, advancing an argument that resonates in the twenty-first century: "All experience shows that crime has not increased, but diminished, as the criminal laws of a country have become less barbarous and vindictive."

Jenison's initiative was rejected, after which Vermont averaged an execution about every five years until 1954, when the last occurred—that of Donald Demag, for escaping from prison, breaking into a home, and killing a woman.

A decade later, the state legislature abolished capital punishment for all crimes except a murder following a prior unrelated murder and the murder of a prison guard by a prisoner serving a life sentence.

When there had been no crime meeting those criteria by 1987, the last vestige of capital punishment was removed from state statutes.

While serendipity intervened to save the Boorns and scores of other innocent men and women from the worst mistake known to law, it has not, alas, saved them all.

At least two innocent men were denied the luck of the Boorns. One was William Jackson Marion, who was hanged in 1887 in Nebraska for the murder of John Cameron. The other was Charles Hudspeth, who was hanged five years later in Arkansas for the murder of George Watkins. The innocence of Marion and Watkins came to light when their presumed victims turned up alive and well after the hangings (see "Other Dead Alive Cases"). Probably hundreds of others—among more than fifteen thousand men and women executed under civil authority since the founding of Jamestown—were just as innocent as Marion and Watkins, although precisely how many and precisely which ones they were will never be known.

There is no question that twentieth-century scientific and legal advances—particularly DNA forensic technology and Warren Court decisions defining the rights of the accused—reduced the U.S. wrongful execution rate.

Without a healthy dose of good luck, however, few of the modern wrongfully condemned would have escaped execution. A telling example is the case of Anthony Porter, an Illinois death row prisoner who was saved from execution in 1998 by his low IQ. Although it was then legal to execute the mentally retarded—the U.S. Supreme Court would not ban the practice until 2000—the law required that a defendant at least understand what was about to happen to him and why. Porter had scored so low on an IQ test that it was unclear whether he met that criterion. The Illinois Supreme Court, consequently, granted a reprieve for additional IQ testing, which opened the window for a team of Northwestern University journalism students to reinvestigate the case and establish Porter's innocence.

And another example is the case of Gary Drinkard, who was saved from execution in Alabama by his bad back. Drinkard had been sentenced to death for the 1993 murder of a Decatur junk dealer, but his conviction was reversed for ineffective assistance of counsel. He was exonerated in 2001 after two physicians testified that his back condition was so severe at the time of the crime that it was impossible for him to have committed it.

And in Maryland, Kirk Bloodsworth might well have been executed for the murder of a nine-year-old girl—a crime for which he was sentenced to death in 1985—had not DNA forensic technology happened

<143>

along. In 1992, Bloodsworth became the first death row prisoner to be exonerated by DNA, which, twelve years later, identified the child's actual killer.

Such near misses give rise to a strong inference that other modern mistakes must have eluded detection and that innocent persons must have been executed. Yet it has not been proven that any innocent person has been executed under death penalty laws enacted in the wake of the U.S. Supreme Court's 1972 decision in *Furman v. Georgia.*

Why, if proof exists, has it been so elusive?

The reason is that once an execution occurs, avenues for pursuing claims of actual innocence are closed.

In at least three cases, courts have refused to allow DNA testing that stood to exonerate an executed prisoner.

The first case was that of Roger Coleman, a coal miner convicted of the 1981 rape and murder of his sister-in-law. As the execution neared, Coleman's lawyers won an order allowing DNA testing on a vaginal swab.

The testing was performed by a pioneering forensic geneticist, Edward T. Blake, who concluded that Coleman was among about 2 percent of the population who could have been the source of semen on the swab. In other words, there was 98 percent probability that Coleman was guilty.

If a 98 percent probability of guilt were an appropriate standard, it would mean that eighteen of those executed following *Furman* were innocent. But it was good enough for Governor Douglas Wilder, who dispatched Coleman to the Virginia electric chair.

Coleman's last words were, "An innocent man is going to be murdered tonight."

Eight years after the execution, Blake informed the trial judge that DNA technology had advanced to the point where it might be possible to establish with certainty whether the semen had been Coleman's, but the judge refused to allow retesting.

Centurion Ministries, a New Jersey–based organization dedicated to rectifying wrongful convictions, and four newspapers filed suit, but the Virginia Supreme Court threw out the case.

In the second case, which also occurred in Virginia, a man named Joseph O'Dell was executed in 1997 for the murder a dozen years earlier of a woman who had been abducted, beaten with the butt of a rifle, raped, and strangled.

Shortly after the crime, O'Dell appeared at a convenience store drenched in blood. He said he had been in a fight, and witnesses verified that. Because DNA testing had not yet become a standard practice, a forensics lab could only offer that the blood on his clothes was "consistent" with the victim's.

Years later, after exhausting his appeals, O'Dell sought a court order for DNA testing of a vaginal swab taken from the victim and of the blood on his clothes.

<145>

Although such testing had the potential to prove his innocence, the court refused to permit it.

O'Dell went to his death insisting, "Governor, you're killing the wrong man."

In an effort to determine the truth, the Roman Catholic Diocese of Richmond filed suit demanding the testing. The prosecution argued that if the requested testing turned out to be exculpatory, "it would be shouted from the rooftops that the Commonwealth of Virginia executed an innocent man."

The court ordered the evidence destroyed.

The third case was that of Richard Wayne Jones, who was executed in Texas in 1999 for the murder of a housewife thirteen years earlier. An apparently random victim, the woman had been abducted and her car commandeered from a parking lot near Fort Worth. She was robbed, stabbed nineteen times, and set afire.

There was no question that Jones had something to do with the crime—his fingerprint was found in the victim's car—but it was not until 1987, six years after his conviction, that he told his side of the story.

He claimed he had only helped dispose of the body after his drug-addled sister, Brenda Jones, and her boyfriend, Walter Sellers, committed the murder. They denied the crime, but two witnesses came forward to claim that Sellers, who by this time was in prison for mail theft, had told them Jones was innocent. And three other witnesses reported that they had seen Sellers with stolen checks and blood on his clothes about the time of the crime.

More important, there was physical evidence that could be tested for DNA—eight cigarette butts recovered from the car. Since the victim did not smoke and Jones smoked a different brand, the butts suggested that someone else had been involved.

Yet the Texas courts refused to allow DNA testing, and Jones went to his death proclaiming, "I want the victim's family to know I did not commit this crime."

Jones left two adult sons, who filed a civil action seeking DNA testing on the butts in the hope of clearing their father's name, but the judge refused. The sons considered an appeal but abandoned the idea as hopeless and dropped the case, removing the only legal impediment to the destruction of the evidence that might have corroborated their father's claim of innocence.

The cases against Coleman, O'Dell, and Jones were no stronger than those against Drinkard, Bloodsworth, Porter—and the Boorns.

The different outcomes, it would appear, were simply the result of bad and good luck.

<147>

Stephen Boorn's Written Confession

Below is an annotated text of Stephen Boorn's written confession, dated August 27, 1819, to the murder of Russell Colvin on May 10, 1812.

May the tenth, 1812, I, about nine or ten o'clock, went down to David Glazier's bridge, and fished down below uncle Nathaniel Boorn's, and then went up across their farms, where Russell and Lewis was, being the nighest way, and sat down and began to talk, and Russell told me how many dollars benefit he had been to father, and I told him he was a damned fool, and he was mad and jumped up, and we sat close together, and I told him to set down, you little tory, and there was a piece of a beech limb about two feet long, and he catched it up and struck at my head as I sat down, and I jumpt up and it struck me on the shoulder, and I catched it out of his hand and struck him a back handed blow, I being on the north side of him, and there was a knot on it about one inch long.

<148>

As I struck him I did think I hit him on his back, and he stooped down and that knot was broken off sharp, and it hit him on the back of the neck, close in his hair, and it went in about a half an inch on that great cord, and he fell down, and then I told the boy to go down and come up with his uncle John,[1] and he asked me if I had killed Russell, and I told him no, but he must not tell that we struck one another. And I told him, when he got away down, Russell was gone away, and I went back and he was dead, and then I went and took him and put him in the corner of the fence by the cellar hole, and put briars over him and went home and went down to the barn and got some boards, and when it was dark I went down and took a hoe and boards, and dug a grave as well as I could, and took out of his pocket a little barlow knife,[2] with about a half of a blade, and cut some bushes and put on his face and the boards, and put in the grave, and put him in four boards, on the bottom, and on the top, and t'other two on the sides, and then covered him up, and went home crying along, but I want afraid as I know on. And when I lived at William Boorn's[3] I planted some potatoes, and when I dug them I went there and something I thought had been there, I took up his bones and put them in a basket, and took the boards and put on my potato hole, and then it was night, took the basket and my hoe and went down and pulled a plank in the stable[4] floor, and then dug a hole, and then covered him up, and went in the house and told them I had done with the bas-

<149>

ket and took back the shovel, and covered up my potatoes that evening, and then when I lived under the west
mountain,[5] Lewis came and told me that father's barn
was burnt up, the next day or the next day but one, I came
down and went to the barn and there was a few bones,
and when they was to dinner I told them I did not want
my dinner, and went and took them, and there want only
a few of the biggest bones, and throwed them in the river
above Wyman's,[6] and then went back, and it was done
quick too, and then was hungry by that time, and then
went home, and the next Sunday I came down after
money to pay the boot[7] that I gave to boot between ox-
ens, and went out there and scraped up them little things
that was under the stump there, and told them I was going to fishing, and went, and there was a hole, and I
dropped them in and kicked over the stuff, and that is the
first any body knew it, either friends or foes, even my
wife. And these I acknowledge before the world.

STEPHEN BOORN

MANCHESTER, AUGUST 27, 1819

Notes
1. Older brother of Stephen and Jesse Boorn.
2. A pocketknife manufactured in Sheffield, England, specifically
for export to the United States from the late 1700s through the
early 1900s.
3. William Boorn was Stephen's first cousin and owner of a farm
where Stephen lived and was seasonally employed.

<150>

4. Also known as a sheep barn.

5. On the farm purchased with the proceeds of the 1815 sale to Thomas Johnson of the parcel of land where the murder was believed to have occurred.

6. The Battenkill River, north of a farm owned by William Wyman.

7. Apparently a reference to shoeing oxen.

<151>

The Boorn brothers were the first of eleven wrongfully convicted defendants in "dead alive" cases known to have occurred in the United States. Below are summaries of the other cases.

Louise Butler and George Yelder

In early April 1928, in Lowndes County, Alabama, Louise Butler came to suspect her paramour, George Yelder, of knowing, in the biblical sense, her fourteen-year-old niece, Topsy Warren. After returning from a trip to Montgomery one day, Butler jealously confronted Topsy with her suspicion. Topsy thereupon vanished, and the county sheriff came to suspect foul play.

During questioning, three children—Topsy's nine-year-old sister and two younger cousins—purportedly claimed that Louise and George together had murdered Topsy. The story the sheriff attributed to the children was exceedingly gruesome: Butler supposedly struck Topsy

<152>

with an ax, with which Yelder dismembered the corpse. The remains allegedly were put into a sack, which Butler and Yelder threw into the Alabama River.

Based on the children's accounts, Butler—but, inexplicably, not Yelder—was arrested. After a few days in jail, Butler orally confessed. Her confession, which she soon recanted, matched what the children had said, according to the sheriff. On April 17, 1928, less than two weeks after Topsy disappeared, Butler and Yelder were indicted by a grand jury. Only a week later, they were tried separately before Judge A. E. Gamble. Each trial lasted less than a day, Butler's on April 24 and Yelder's on April 25. Judge Gamble suppressed Butler's confession, based on her recantation, but the children repeated the hair-raising tale they had told the sheriff. The defendants testified at their respective trials, denying knowledge of Topsy's disappearance. The juries, which then by law were all white in Alabama, promptly returned verdicts of guilty. On April 25, Judge Gamble sentenced the defendants to life in prison.

Less than a week later, Topsy was discovered alive, well, and residing less than twenty miles away, her limbs intact. In June 1928, Butler and Yelder were officially exonerated and released. The children then admitted that they had fabricated the story, at the behest of a man who had a grievance against Yelder. It was never explained why they also had implicated Butler or why she had confessed.

Condy Dabney

When a girl's body was found in a mine shaft near Coxton, Kentucky, in September 1925, the authorities claimed it was that of fourteen-year-old Mary Vickery, who had disappeared the previous August 23. In March 1926, Condy Dabney, a married father of two and former miner who had forsaken that occupation to become a cabdriver, was indicted for her murder.

The charges stemmed from allegations made by another girl, Marie Jackson, who came forward six months after the crime claiming to have been an eyewitness to the murder. The morning of the purported crime, Marie said she and Mary hailed Dabney's cab. The three went to a restaurant and, a little later, to a secluded area, where Dabney made sexual advances toward Mary. When Mary protested, Dabney struck her with a stick and she fell to the ground. Marie tried to hide, but Dabney found her. He forced her to accompany him to the mine, where they dumped Mary's body. Marie had not come forward earlier, she said, because Dabney threatened to burn her at the stake, or to have a friend do it, if she told anyone about the crime.

The prosecution's case was not strong. At Dabney's trial, which occurred less than a month after his indictment, five witnesses substantially contradicted Marie regarding the time of the alleged crime. Marie claimed to have been with Mary and Dabney from seven A.M. until dark, but three friends of Mary's claimed to have been

<154>

with her during the afternoon. The friends said a man named William Middleton had given them and Mary a ride that afternoon, and their account was corroborated by the mother of two of the girls and by Middleton.

The identification of the body also was dubious. It was too badly decomposed for anyone to identify it by appearance, and the defense insisted that the decomposition was too extensive for the body to be that of someone who had been dead only a little more than a month. A ring and stocking that the prosecution claimed had been found with the body were identified as Mary's by her father, but his testimony was impeached because he did not attend the funeral. On cross-examination, he acknowledged that after viewing the body, he had not been "perfectly sure" it was his daughter's. Moreover, although the father claimed the hair matched Mary's hair, which was light, two other witnesses who had seen the body claimed the hair was dark. Exhumation could have resolved the issue, but that apparently was not suggested.

To bolster the prosecution's weak case, a jailhouse informant was called to the stand. His name was Claude Scott, and he happened to be an acquaintance of Marie Jackson's. Scott claimed that Dabney had offered him fifteen dollars to falsely testify that Marie had admitted concocting the murder tale. It was not established whether the prosecution rewarded Scott for his testimony. Dabney took the stand in his own defense. He said he had no recollection of ever having had Mary Vickery in his cab,

<155>

although Marie Jackson had been a customer on several occasions.

Despite the conflicting evidence, the jury convicted Dabney on March 31, 1926, and the judge sentenced him to life at hard labor. Just a few days short of a year later, while Dabney's appeal was pending, a police officer in Williamsburg, Kentucky, some eighty-five miles west of Coxton, happened to notice the name Mary Vickery on a hotel register. Because the name seemed familiar, he spoke with her and soon learned that she was the person Dabney had been convicted of killing. She said she had run away the year before because she wasn't getting along with her stepmother. Mary said she did not even know Marie Jackson, who admitted she had concocted the story to collect a five-hundred-dollar reward posted by Mary's father. Jackson was convicted of perjury on March 27, 1927. The body from the mine apparently was never identified.

Charles Hudspeth

George Watkins and his wife, Rebecca, moved in 1886 from Kansas to Marion County, Arkansas, where Rebecca apparently soon became intimately involved with Charles Hudspeth. The following year, Watkins disappeared.

Rebecca and Hudspeth were arrested, and after lengthy interrogation, Rebecca allegedly made a state-

<156>

ment accusing Hudspeth of murdering Watkins to get him out of the way so they could be married.

Based on Rebecca's testimony, Hudspeth was convicted and sentenced to death, but the Arkansas Supreme Court set aside the conviction on the ground that the trial judge, R. H. Powell, had improperly barred testimony regarding Rebecca's alleged lack of good character.

Upon retrial, Hudspeth was again convicted and again sentenced to death. He was hanged at Harrison, Arkansas, on December 30, 1892, but in June 1893, Hudspeth's lawyer, W. F. Pace, located Watkins alive and well in Kansas.

William Jackson Marion

William Jackson Marion and John Cameron, who boarded together in Clay County, Kansas, journeyed in May 1872 to Gage County, Nebraska, to visit John and Rachel Warren, Marion's in-laws. The day before they left Kansas, Marion purportedly signed a contract to purchase a team of horses from Cameron for $315, paying $30 down. It was agreed that Cameron would keep the horses until Marion paid the balance. Marion and Cameron left the Warren place in mid-May, saying they were heading west to work on the railroad. A few days later, Marion returned alone to Gage County.

Eleven years later, a body was found on a former Otoe and Missouri Indian reservation dressed in cloth-

<157>

ing that witnesses identified as Cameron's. Marion was indicted, convicted, and sentenced to death for murder. However, the Nebraska Supreme Court reversed and remanded the case for a new trial because Marion had been sentenced by a judge rather than a jury. At the time of the crime, the law required jury sentencing, although by the time of the trial the law had been changed to allow sentencing by a judge.

Marion was promptly retried, convicted, and sentenced to death, this time by a jury—a result that the state high court affirmed. He went to the gallows on March 25, 1887, proclaiming—as he had from the beginning—that he was innocent.

Four years later, Cameron turned up alive. He explained that he had absconded to Mexico in 1872 to avoid a shotgun wedding in Kansas. On the centennial of Marion's execution—March 25, 1987—Nebraska governor Bob Kerrey granted William Jackson Marion, posthumously, a full pardon based on innocence.

Antonio Rivera and Merla Walpole

When the body of a little girl was found near San Bernardino, California, in 1973, the authorities concluded that it was that of three-year-old Judy Rivera, whose parents had been suspected of killing her eight years earlier.

When the parents, Antonio Rivera and Merla Walpole, went on trial in March 1973, they told a sad story. In

<158>

1965, Rivera was unable to support the family, and Judy was seriously ill. In desperation, Rivera and Walpole decided to abandon the child, in the hope that she might receive the care she needed. So that she could not be traced back to them, they drove to San Francisco and left her at a filling station, where, the *San Francisco Chronicle* reported the next day, the little girl was found. The jury didn't believe them, however, and returned a verdict of guilty.

But before sentencing, Judge Thomas M. Haldorsen set aside the verdict, ordered a new trial, and directed the prosecution to investigate the defendants' claim. In October 1975, Timothy Martin, an investigator for the district attorney's office, located the little girl, who had been left in San Francisco a decade earlier. Now thirteen, she strongly resembled Rivera and Walpole. After blood tests and comparisons of bone formations indicated she in all likelihood was their daughter, the prosecution dropped the charges. The body found in 1973 was never identified.

James Smith

After the congregation of a small church in Reid's Ferry, Virginia, voted in July 1908 to replace their pastor, the Reverend James Smith, with a younger man, the Reverend Ernest Lyons, the reverends got into a quarrel over forty-five dollars, and the latter threatened to kill the former. A few days later, on August 1, Smith failed to ap-

<159>

pear at a church conference in nearby Suffolk, arousing suspicions among his church allies that Lyons had made good on the threat.

When, a few months after Smith disappeared, news reached Reid's Ferry that a body of a man generally fitting Smith's description had been found in the Nansemond River near Suffolk, Smith's supporters were convinced their suspicions were correct. They contacted Commonwealth Attorney James U. Burgess, who arranged for the body from the river to be exhumed. It was bloated and in an advanced state of decomposition, but a ring on the little finger of the left hand appeared to match one that Smith was known to have owned. The clothing on the corpse also matched descriptions provided by persons familiar with Smith's wardrobe. An autopsy determined that the man had been struck in the head with a dull instrument and thrown into the river when he was dead or dying. When questioned about the murder, Lyons lied, claiming to have seen Smith recently in Newport News, Norfolk, and Portsmouth.

Lyons was indicted for first-degree murder, carrying the death penalty. At a three-day trial, which began on January 13, 1909, in Suffolk, several members of the church testified about the death threat Lyons had leveled at Smith the previous year. Lyons's lawyer, Robert W. Withers, contended that the corpse was not Smith's and, in any event, the evidence was insufficient to connect Lyons to Smith's disappearance. The jury disagreed but

<160>

found Lyons guilty only of the lesser included offense of second-degree murder, apparently having concluded that Smith's death resulted from a renewed outbreak of the quarrel over the forty-five dollars and therefore that the death penalty was not appropriate. Judge James L. McLemore sentenced Lyons to eighteen years in prison.

After a motion for a new trial was denied, Withers, believing strongly in his client's innocence, pleaded with Judge McLemore to reconsider and at least grant a hearing on the motion. McLemore agreed to the hearing, only on the condition that Withers first go to Lyons, tell him that the motion had been denied, and ask what really happened. When Withers did so, he found Lyons no longer maintaining his innocence. Lyons said he indeed had been involved in the crime but had not committed it alone. Smith's death, he said, was a result of conspiracy involving several members of the congregation—specifically those who had testified for the prosecution at the trial. Lyons promptly recanted the allegation, but this latest lie, on top of those he had earlier told, sealed his fate. He went to the penitentiary.

Three years later, the clerk of the Nansemond County Circuit Court, George E. Bunting, discovered Smith living in good health in North Carolina and, incidentally, wearing on the little finger of his left hand a ring like the one found on the corpse from the river. Smith voluntarily returned to Suffolk, where at a hearing before Judge McLemore his identity was confirmed by mem-

<161>

bers of his church. Smith acknowledged that he had read newspaper stories about Lyons's trial and conviction but had done nothing because he feared prosecution for absconding with church funds—the forty-five dollars over which the reverends had quarreled. The corpse from the river was never identified.

Bill Wilson

In the spring of 1912, a father and son fishing along the Warrior River in Blount County, Alabama, noticed a bone protruding from a bluff. Clearing away the soil, they uncovered what appeared to be the remains of an adult and a child. As news of the discovery spread, a number of area residents, presuming the remains to be ancient, visited the bluff in the hope of finding Indian relics.

When no relics were found, a farmworker named Jim House began speculating that the remains were not Indian but those of Jenny Wade Wilson and her nineteen-month-old child, who had disappeared after Jenny obtained a divorce from Bill Wilson in late 1908. House also belatedly asserted that shortly after the divorce, he had seen Jenny go into her former in-laws' home carrying a basket. The next day, House said, he noticed footprints leading toward the river and found what he described as a "child's cloth" and blood on a rock.

Blount County solicitor James Embry was sufficiently impressed by House's tale that he obtained a

<162>

grand jury indictment charging Wilson with murdering Jenny and the child. After his arrest, Wilson encountered in jail an ex-convict, Mack Holcomb, who later claimed that he overheard Wilson tell a relative during a visit, "If you tell anything I will tend to you when I get out." Other witnesses claimed that after the divorce Wilson vowed to kill Jenny if he ever saw her again. Embry's case was weakened by the testimony of the prosecution medical expert, Dr. Marvin Denton, who acknowledged that it was unlikely, although perhaps not impossible, that the skeletal remains from the bluff could have deteriorated to the extent they had in just five years. Furthermore, Denton acknowledged, the skull of the child had second teeth, which usually do not develop until about age four.

The defense case, in contrast, was strong. Six witnesses, including Jenny's sister, testified that they had seen Jenny at various times several months after she should have been dead, assuming the prosecution theory was correct. Four relatives of Wilson's, and Wilson himself, denied House's contention that Jenny had come to Wilson's parents' home after the divorce. Finally, a defense medical expert, Dr. J. E. Hancock, testified that the teeth in the adult skull were those of an elderly person and that a nineteen-month-old child would not have second teeth. Nonetheless, the jury found Wilson guilty, and Judge J. E. Blackwood sentenced him to life in prison on December 18, 1915.

After the trial, further doubt was cast on the verdict

<163>

when Dr. Alex Hrdlicka, curator of physical anthropology at the Smithsonian Institution in Washington, D.C., examined the bones from the bluff and declared them to be very old skeletal parts of four or more persons. Judge Blackwood concluded that justice had miscarried, but he no longer had jurisdiction of the case. Thus, he asked the governor to grant clemency effecting Wilson's release. Before the governor took action, however, Wilson's appellate lawyer located Jenny and her child, now eleven, living in Vincennes, Indiana. She returned to Blount County on July 8, 1918, and the same day, after authorities confirmed her identity, the governor granted Wilson a pardon.

<164>

Below is a list of defendants sentenced to death and exonerated in the United States as of January 1, 2005. Names in bold are those of defendants who falsely confessed or made statements construed as confessions or who were convicted in part based on codefendants' or alternative suspects' false statements. Names in italic are those of defendants against whom in-custody informants (jailhouse snitches, in the vernacular) or other incentivized witnesses—in some cases the persons later shown to have committed the crime—claimed either to have heard the defendant make a statement indicative of guilt or to have witnessed the crime. Names in bold italic are those of defendants whose cases fall into both categories. In parenthesis are the year of arrest, year of release, and the state in which the conviction occurred.

Randall Dale Adams (1976, 1989, Tex.)
Joseph Amrine (1985, 2003, Mo.)
Alf Banks Jr. (1919, 1923, Ark.)

<*165*>

Jerry Banks (1974, 1980, Ga.)

Joseph Barbato (1929, 1931, N.Y.)

Gary L. Beeman (1976, 1979, Ohio)

Thomas Berdue (1851, 1851, Calif.)

Charles Bernstein (1933, 1945, D.C.)

Jerry D. Bigelow (1980, 1988, Calif.)

Kirk N. Bloodsworth (1984, 1993, Md.)

Jesse Boorn (1819, 1820, Vt.)

Stephen Boorn (1819, 1820, Vt.)

Clifford H. Bowen (1980, 1986, Okla.)

Joe Bowles (1919, 1921, N.C.)

Thomas Bram (1896, 1919, Mass.)

Clarence Brandley (1980, 1990, Tex.)

Joseph Briggs (1905, 1905, Ill.)

Dan L. Bright (1996, 2004, La.)

Coke Brite (1936, 1951, Calif.)

John H. Brite (1936, 1951, Calif.)

Anthony Silah Brown (1983, 1986, Fla.)

J. B. Brown (1901, 1913, Fla.)

Jesse Keith Brown (1983, 1989, S.C.)

Shabaka Brown (1974, 1987, Fla.)

Willie A. Brown (1983, 1987, Fla.)

Harry D. Bundy (1957, 1958, Ohio)

Albert Ronnie Burrell (1986, 2000, La.)

Joseph Burrows (1988, 1994, Ill.)

Sabrina Butler (1989, 1995, Miss.)

Harry F. Cashin (1931, 1933, N.Y.)

Gangi Cero (1927, 1930, Mass.)

Izell Chambers (1933, 1942, Fla.)
Earl Patrick Charles (1974, 1978, Ga.)
Eric Clemmons (1989, 2000, Mo.)
Perry Cobb (1977, 1986, Ill.)
James W. Cochran, (1977, 1997, Ala.)
Ed Coleman (1919, 1923, Ark.)
Kerry Max Cook (1997, 1999, Tex.)
Tony Cooks (1980, 1986, Calif.)
Ralph Cooper (1948, 1951, N.J.)
Robert C. Cox (1986, 1989, Fla.)
James Creamer (1974, 1975, Ga.)
Patrick Croy (1978, 1990, Calif.)
Robert C. Cruz (1980, 1993, Ariz.)
Rolando Cruz (1983, 1995, Ill.)
Frank Davino (1938, 1942, N.Y.)
Charlie Davis (1933, 1942, Fla.)
Muneer Deeb (1982, 1993, Tex.)
Clarence R. Dexter Jr. (1990, 1999, Mo.)
Robert K. Domer (1963, 1971, Ohio)
Frank Dove (1922, 1928, N.C.)
Fred Dove (1922, 1928, N.C.)
Henry A. Drake (1977, 1987, Ga.)
Ayliff Draper (1935, 1936, Ark.)
Gary Drinkard (1993, 2001, Ala.)
Collis English (1948, 1951, N.J.)
Charles I. Fain (1983, 2001, Idaho)
Neil Ferber (1981, 1986, Pa.)
McKinley Forrest (1948, 1951, N.J.)

James F. Foster (1956, 1958, Ga.)

Joe Fox (1919, 1923, Ark.)

Leo Frank (1913, 1918, Ga.)

Gary Gauger (1994, 1996, Ill.)

Allen Gell (1995, 2004, N.C.)

Charles R. Giddens (1978, 1982, Okla.)

Albert Giles (1919, 1923, Ark.)

James Giles (1961, 1967, Md.)

John Giles (1961, 1967, Md.)

Thomas V. Gladish (1974, 1976, N.Mex.)

Andrew Lee Golden (1989, 1993, Fla.)

Ernest Shujaa Graham (1973, 1981, Calif.)

Michael R. Graham (1986, 2000, La.)

David W. Grannis (1989, 1996, Ariz.)

Louis Greco (1965, 2001, Mass.)

Joseph Nahume Green (1992, 1999, Fla.)

Nelson Green (1915, 1918, N.Y.)

Richard W. Greer (1974, 1976, N.Mex.)

Ricardo Aldape Guerra (1982, 1997, Tex.)

Ernest Haines (1916, 1918, Pa.)

Paul Hall (1919, 1923, Ark.)

Benjamin H. Harris III (1984, 1997, Wash.)

L. D. Harris (1947, 1957, S.C.)

Robert Hayes (1991, 1997, Fla.)

Timothy B. Hennis (1986, 1989, N.C.)

Alejandro Hernandez (1983, 1995, Ill.)

Ed Hicks (1919, 1923, Ark.)

Frank Hicks (1919, 1923, Ark.)

Larry Hicks (1978, 1980, Ind.)
Madison Hobley (1987, 2003, Ill.)
Rudolph Holton (1986, 2003, Fla.)
Stanley Howard (1984, 2003, Ill.)
Timothy Howard (1976, 2003, Ohio)
Charles Hudspeth (1887, 1892, Ark.)
Paul Kern Imbler (1961, 1971, Calif.)
Sonia Jacobs (1976, 1992, Fla.)
Gary L. James (1976, 2003, Ohio)
Anibal Jaramillo (1981, 1982, Fla.)
Jasper Jenkins (1906, 1907, Oreg.)
William Riley Jent (1980, 1988, Fla.)
Verneal Jimerson (1985, 1996, Ill.)
Cooper Johnson (1922, 1923, Tex.)
Joseph Johnson Jr. (1961, 1967, Md.)
Lawyer Johnson (1971, 1982, Mass.)
Dale N. Johnston (1982, 1990, Ohio)
Richard N. Jones (1983, 1987, Okla.)
Ronald Jones (1985, 1999, Ill.)
Tom Jones (1936, 1943, Ky.)
Troy Lee Jones (1982, 1996, Calif.)
Theodore V. Jordan (1932, 1964, Oreg.)
David R. Keaton (1971, 1973, Fla.)
Ronald B. Keine (1974, 1976, N.Mex.)
Robert Lee Kidd (1960, 1961, Calif.)
Thomas Kimbell Jr. (1996, 2002, Pa.)
John H. Knapp (1974, 1987, Ariz.)
J. E. Knox (1919, 1923, Ark.)

Ray Kronc (1991, 2002, Ariz.)
Curtis L. Kyles (1984, 1998, La.)
David Lamson (1933, 1934, Calif.)
Gus C. Langley (1932, 1936, N.C.)
Edward Larkman (1925, 1933, N.Y.)
Carl Lawson (1989, 1996, Ill.)
Chol Soo Lee (1974, 1983, Calif.)
Wilbert Lee (1963, 1975, Fla.)
George Lettrich (1950, 1953, Ill.)
Camilo Leyra (1950, 1956, N.Y.)
Peter J. Limone (1965, 2001, Mass.)
Michael Linder (1979, 1981, S.C.)
Ralph W. Lobaugh (1947, 1977, Ind.)
Max Ludkowitz (1934, 1935, N.Y.)
Allison M. MacFarland (1912, 1913, N.J.)
Federico M. Macias (1984, 1993, Tex.)
Steve Manning (1990, 2000, Ill.)
Warren D. Manning (1988, 1999, S.C.)
Alvin Mansell (1925, 1930, N.C.)
William Jackson Marion (1883, 1887, Nebr.)
John Martin (1919, 1923, Ark.)
Joaquin Jose Martinez (1996, 2001, Fla.)
Pietro Matera (1931, 1960, N.Y.)
Jimmy Lee Mathers (1987, 1990, Ariz.)
Ryan Matthews (1977, 2004, La.)
John McKenzie (1948, 1951, N.J.)
Vernon McManus (1976, 1987, Tex.)
Walter McMillian (1987, 1993, Ala.)

Juan Roberto Melendez (1983, 2002, Fla.)

Earnest Lee Miller (1980, 1988, Fla.)

Henry W. Miller (1877, 1902, Kans.)

Lloyd E. Miller Jr. (1955, 1971, Ill.)

Robert L. Miller Jr. (1986, 1998, Okla.)

Roberto Miranda (1982, 1996, Nev.)

Olen Montgomery (1932, 1943, Ala.)

Thomas J. Mooney (1913, 1939, Calif.)

Frank Moore (1919, 1923, Ark.)

Gordon Morris (1953, 1976, Tex.)

Oscar L. Morris (1982, 2000, Calif.)

Charles Munsey (1993, 1999, N.C.)

Adolph H. Munson (1984, 1995, Okla.)

Gary X. Nelson (1980, 1991, Ga.)

William Nieves (1992, 2000, Pa.)

Clarence Norris (1931, 1943, Ala.)

Leroy Orange (1984, 2003, Ill.)

Larry Osborne (1999, 2002, Ky.)

Randall Padgett (1990, 1997, Ala.)

Donald Paradis (1980, 2001, Idaho)

Lemuel Parrott (1947, 1948, N.C.)

Aaron Patterson (1986, 2003, Ill.)

Anthony R. Peek (1978, 1987, Fla.)

John Pender (1914, 1920, Oreg.)

Richard Phillips (1900, 1930, Va.)

Freddie Lee Pitts (1963, 1975, Fla.)

Samuel A. Poole (1973, 1974, N.C.)

Anthony Porter (1982, 1999, Ill.)

<171>

Lemuel Prion (1992, 2003, Ariz.)
Will Purvis (1893, 1898, Miss.)
Harry Pyle (1935, 1945, Kans.)
Juan Florencio Ramos (1983, 1987, Fla.)
Ralph Reno (1925, 1928, Ill.)
James J. Richardson (1967, 1989, Fla.)
Alfred Rivera (1996, 1999, N.C.)
Willie Roberson (1931, 1937, Ala.)
James Robison (1976, 1993, Ariz.)
Courtney Rogers (1941, 1943, Calif.)
Johnny Ross (1975, 1981, La.)
John Edward Schuyler (1907, 1914, N.J.)
Bradley P. Scott (1988, 1991, Fla.)
Howard Shaffer (1927, 1930, Fla.)
Jeremy Sheets (1997, 2001, Ind.)
David Sherman (1907, 1911, Tenn.)
John C. Skelton (1982, 1990, Tex.)
Charles Smith (1983, 1991, Ind.)
Clarence Smith Jr. (1974, 1976, N.Mex.)
Frank Lee Smith (1985, 2000, Fla.)
Jay C. Smith (1985, 1992, Pa.)
Steven Smith (1985, 1999, Ill.)
Christopher Spicer (1973, 1974, N.C.)
F. N. Staples (1905, 1905, Calif.)
Gordon Steidl (1987, 2004, Ill.)
Charles Stevens (1927, 1930, Fla.)
Charles F. Stielow (1915, 1918, N.Y.)
Michael J. Synon (1900, 1902, Ill.)

Henry Tameleo (1965, 2001, Mass.)
John Thompson (1985, 2003, La.)
James Thorpe (1948, 1951, N.J.)
Delbert Tibbs (1974, 1976, Fla.)
Darby Tillis (1977, 1986, Ill.)
Andrew Toth (1891, 1911, Pa.)
Jonathan C. Treadway Jr. (1975, 1978, Ariz.)
William Troop (1927, 1930, Fla.)
Larry Troy (1983, 1987, Fla.)
John Valletutti (1947, 1949, N.Y.)
Earnest Wallace (1916, 1918, Ill.)
Robert Wallace (1979, 1987, Ga.)
Lewis Wallenberger (1860, 1861, N.J.)
Zian Sung Wan (1919, 1926, D.C.)
Ed Ware (1919, 1923, Ark.)
Earl Washington Jr. (1983, 2000, Va.)
Joseph Weaver (1927, 1929, Ohio)
Dick Weldon (1892, 1895, Ga.)
William M. Wellman (1942, 1943, N.C.)
Gregory R. Wilhoit (1986, 1993, Okla.)
Dennis Williams (1978, 1996, Ill.)
Eugene Williams (1931, 1937, Ala.)
George Williams (1922, 1928, N.C.)
Samuel Tito Williams (1948, 1963, N.Y.)
Jack Williamson (1933, 1942, Fla.)
Ronald K. Williamson (1982, 1999, Okla.)
Ernest Ray Willis (1996, 2004, Tex.)
Horace Wilson (1948, 1951, N.J.)

<173>

William Woods (1877, 1889, Kans.)
Walter Woodward (1933, 1944, Fla.)
Lem Woon (1908, 1935, Oreg.)
Will Wordlow (1919, 1923, Ark.)
Nicholas J. Yarris (1981, 2003, Pa.)
Bennie Young (1922, 1934, Tex.)
Herman Zajicek (1908, 1916, Ill.)
Isidore Zimmerman (1938, 1962, N.Y.)

Defendants wrongfully sentenced to death: 235
Convicted in whole or part on false admissions: 59
Convicted in whole or part on informant testimony: 79
Convicted on both false admissions and informant testimony: 14
Convicted on false admissions, informant testimony, or both: 124

Bibliography

Atkins v. Virginia, 536 U.S. 304 (2002).

Borchard, Edwin. *Convicting the Innocent.* New Haven, Conn.: Yale University Press, 1932.

Brandon, Ruth, and Christie Davies. *Wrongful Imprisonment: Mistaken Convictions and Their Consequences.* Hamden, Conn.: Archon Books, 1973.

Davey, Monica. "Anthony Porter, the Four Walls of His Life." *Chicago Tribune,* July 18, 1999, p. 1.

Enzinna, Paul F. "Afraid of a Shadow of a Doubt." *Washington Post,* May 7, 2000, op-ed page.

Furman v. Georgia, 405 U.S. 912 (1972).

Gerber, Rudolph J. "Death Is Not Worth It." *Arizona State Law Journal* 28 (spring 1996): 335.

Grinstein, Alexander. *Wilkie Collins: Man of Mystery and Imagination.* Madison, Conn.: International Universities Press, 2003.

Hudspeth v. State, 50 Ark. 534 (1888).

<175>

Jones, Lisa. "Vermont and the Death Penalty: How State Lost Its Taste for Vengeance." *Burlington Free Press,* June 10, 2001, p. 1A.

Junkin, Tim. *Bloodsworth: The True Story of the First Death Row Inmate Exonerated by DNA.* Chapel Hill, N.C.: Algonquin Books, 2004.

Leo, Richard, and Richard Ofshe. "The Consequences of False Confessions: Deprivations of Liberty and Miscarriages of Justice in the Age of Psychological Interrogation." *Journal of Criminal Law and Criminology* 88 (spring 1998): 429.

Marion v. Nebraska, 16 Neb. 349 (1884) and 20 Neb. 233 (1886).

McFarland, Gerald W. *The Counterfeit Man: The True Story of the Boorn-Colvin Murder Case.* New York: Pantheon Books, 1990.

Miranda v. Arizona, 384 U.S. 436 (1966).

Moulton, Sherman Roberts. *The Boorn Mystery: An Episode from the Judicial Annals of Vermont.* Barre, Vt.: Vermont Historical Society, 1937.

Mullen, Thomas A. "Rule without Reason: Requiring Independent Proof of the Corpus Delicti as a Condition of Admitting an Extra Judicial Confession." *University of San Francisco Law Review* 27 (winter 1993): 225.

Pearson, Edmund Lester. *Studies in Murder.* Garden City, N.Y.: Garden City Publishing Co., 1924.

<176>

Radelet, Michael L., Hugo Adam Bedau, and Constance E. Putnam. *In Spite of Innocence.* Boston: Northeastern University Press, 1992.

Radin, Edward D. *The Innocents.* New York: William Morrow, 1961.

Romano, Lois. "When DNA Meets Death Row, It's the System That's Tested." *Washington Post,* December 12, 2003, p. A-1.

Roth, Randolph A. "Blood Calls for Vengeance! The History of Capital Punishment in Vermont." *Vermont History* 65 (1997): 10–25.

Sargeant, Leonard. *The Trial, Confessions and Conviction of Jesse and Stephen Boorn for the Murder of Russell Colvin and the Return of the Man Supposed to Have Been Murdered.* Manchester, Vt.: Journal Book and Job Office, 1873.

Scheck, Barry, Peter Neufeld, and Jim Dwyer. *Actual Innocence: Five Days to Execution, and Other Dispatches from the Wrongly Convicted.* New York: Doubleday, 2000.

Spargo, John. *The Return of Russell Colvin.* Bennington, Vt.: Historical Museum and Art Gallery of Bennington, 1945.

Tucker, John C. *May God Have Mercy.* New York: W. W. Norton, 1997.

U.S. v. Singleton, 165 F.3d 1297 (10th Cir. 1999).

Vermont v. Demag, 118 Vt. 273 (1954).

<177>

Waldo, Samuel Putnam. *A Brief Sketch of the Indictment, Trial and Conviction of Stephen and Jesse Boorn.* Hartford, Conn.: Silas Andrus, 1820.

Yant, Martin. *Presumed Guilty.* Buffalo, N.Y.: Prometheus Books, 1991.

<178>

Wilkie Collins (1824–89) was a prominent Victorian novelist and the leading mystery writer of his time. His best-known works are *The Woman in White* and *The Moonstone.*

Rob Warden is the executive director of the Center on Wrongful Convictions at Northwestern University School of Law. An award-winning legal affairs journalist, he is the coauthor with David Protess of *A Promise of Justice* and *Gone in the Night* and was inducted into the Chicago Journalism Hall of Fame in 2004.

Royalties from this book are being donated to the Center on Wrongful Convictions

Northwestern University School of Law
Bluhm Legal Clinic
Center on Wrongful Convictions

MISSION OF THE CENTER

The Center on Wrongful Convictions is dedicated to identifying and rectifying wrongful convictions. The Center has three components: representation, research, and public education. Center faculty, staff, cooperating outside attorneys, and Bluhm Legal Clinic students investigate possible wrongful convictions and represent imprisoned clients with claims of actual innocence or other serious miscarriages of justice. The research and public education components focus on developing initiatives that raise public awareness of the prevalence, causes, and social costs of wrongful convictions and promote substantive reform of the criminal justice system.

www.law.northwestern.edu/wrongfulconvictions